HARLEQUIN®
Presents

To all readers of Harlequin Presents

Thank you for your loyal
custom throughout 2006.

We look forward to bringing you the best
in intense, international and provocatively
passionate romance in 2007.

Happy holidays, and all good wishes
for the New Year!

D0036141

Chantelle Shaw

THE FRENCHMAN'S CAPTIVE WIFE

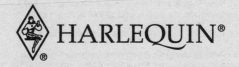

TORONTO • NEW YORK • LONDON
AMSTERDAM • PARIS • SYDNEY • HAMBURG
STOCKHOLM • ATHENS • TOKYO • MILAN • MADRID
PRAGUE • WARSAW • BUDAPEST • AUCKLAND

ISBN-13: 978-0-373-12594-4
ISBN-10:   0-373-12594-1

THE FRENCHMAN'S CAPTIVE WIFE

First North American Publication 2006.

This edition published by arrangement with Harlequin Books S.A.

® and TM are trademarks of the publisher. Trademarks indicated with ® are registered in the United States Patent and Trademark Office, the Canadian Trade Marks Office and in other countries.

www.eHarlequin.com

Printed in U.S.A.

All about the author...
Chantelle Shaw

CHANTELLE SHAW lives on the Kent coast, five minutes from the sea, and does much of her thinking about the characters in her books while walking on the beach. An avid reader from an early age, school friends used to hide their books when she visited, but Chantelle would retreat into her own world, and she still writes "stories" in her head all the time.

Chantelle has been blissfully married to her own tall, dark and very patient hero for over twenty years and has six children. She began to read Harlequin books as a teenager and throughout the years of being a stay-at-home mom to her brood, she found romantic fiction helped her to stay sane!

Her aim is to write books that provide an element of escapism, fun and, of course, romance for the countless women who juggle work and a home-life and who need their precious moments of "me" time. She enjoys reading and writing about strong-willed, feisty women and even stronger-willed sexy heroes. Chantelle is at her happiest when writing. She is particularly inspired while cooking dinner, which unfortunately results in a lot of culinary disasters! She also loves gardening, taking her very badly behaved terrier for walks and eating chocolate (followed by more walking—at least the dog is slim!).

PROLOGUE

August

'OF COURSE WE didn't *bribe* Jean-Luc to marry you!' Sarah Dyer said crisply, 'although I admit there was some financial incentive.'

'Oh, God.' Emily swung away from her mother as a wave of sickness gripped her. Sarah always spent a few weeks of the summer with friends in Hampstead and, although mother and daughter had never been particularly close, she was the first person Emily had turned to in her hour of need. But rather than sympathising, Sarah had unwittingly added the final nail to the coffin. She couldn't stay with Luc now.

'Darling, you have to understand that Jean-Luc Vaillon isn't like other men. You don't amass a multimillion-pound fortune without a ruthless streak, and your husband is first and foremost a businessman.'

'I know,' Emily murmured dully. She didn't need anyone to remind her of Luc's dedication to work, but she was prepared to put up with the endless business trips and the long hours he spent shut away in his study if she thought there was any hope that he might love her.

'The trouble with you, Emily, is that you're a romantic,' Sarah went on, after another glance at her daughter's pale face. 'Perhaps Jean-Luc is having a fling with his personal assistant, but you're his wife and it's in everyone's best interests that you remain so. Pregnancy can place a marriage under huge strain,' she added, eyeing Emily's swollen abdomen, 'and, to put it frankly, I imagine your husband is an extremely virile man. Once the baby's born, everything will return to normal, you'll see.'

But what constituted normal? Emily wondered bleakly as she trudged across the heath, after assuring her mother she would do nothing rash. She had realised soon after her marriage that her role in Luc's life was designated almost exclusively to the bedroom. The fierce sexual attraction that had existed from the moment they had first met was their only real form of communication. Their passion for each other had made them equal but without it they had nothing.

It was busy on the heath. The air rang with children's high-pitched laughter as families took advantage of the late summer sunshine, and as Emily watched a man and a little boy flying a kite, something snapped in her head. She gave a low moan, like an animal in pain, and swiftly covered her mouth with her hands as if she could push the sound back inside. She couldn't fall apart now, not here, but her legs gave way and she sank onto a bench as she faced the reality that her son would never enjoy such an innocent pastime with his father.

She could stay, she thought desperately. For the sake of the baby inside her she could turn a blind eye to the fact that her husband was an unfaithful liar. But Jean-Luc did not want their child any more than he wanted her. His look of horror when he had learned of her pregnancy still haunted her, and his coldness towards her ever since only reinforced her belief that he viewed their marriage as a mistake.

How long had his affair with his personal assistant been going on? she wondered miserably. Robyn Blake had worked for him for years and right from the start she had never missed a chance to emphasise the special relationship she shared with Luc. She was his brother's widow, not just a member of his staff, and Emily had tried to banish her feelings of jealousy at the obvious affection that existed between her husband and his PA. But now she had irrefutable proof that Robyn was Luc's mistress and her sense of betrayal was unbearable.

What about her baby? her mind argued. Her excitement when the ultrasound scan had revealed she was carrying a boy had been overshadowed by misery that Luc hadn't been with her. Of all the hurt he had inflicted on her, that had been the worst, she acknowledged bitterly. He hadn't even bothered to turn up at the hospital to see the magical, grainy image of their child, and she had to face the agonising truth that he just didn't care. Even if she told him he was going to have a son it would make little difference to his attitude. He seemed to grow more and more distant with each passing day and his polite indifference tortured her. Surely it would be better to go now, before her baby was born, and envelop him in her love rather than let him suffer the pain of realising his father had a lump of ice where his heart should be?

Leaving Luc would break her heart, Emily accepted bleakly, but to stay with him now would kill her, and with a muffled sob she stumbled towards the road.

'Where to, love?' the taxi driver asked cheerfully as she climbed into the cab, and for a split second she was torn by indecision, the address of Luc's Chelsea penthouse hovering on her lips.

Maybe she should give him one more chance? Maybe there was a rational explanation why he had spent the night he'd arrived back from Australia with Robyn, rather than returning home to her? But she could not dismiss the images that tortured her mind of Luc making love to his beautiful assistant, and despair overwhelmed her.

Face it, it's over, she told herself savagely, biting down on her lip until her mouth filled with blood. Luc didn't love her and, to give him his due, he had never pretended to. Her mother's revelation that his proposal had been part of a shrewd financial deal only emphasised that fact.

She loved him so much, maybe too much. He was her life, her reason for living, but at that moment the baby kicked and she felt a determined little foot push against her stomach. Now there was a new reason, she reminded herself fiercely, and lifting her chin she relayed the address of her friend Laura's flat to the waiting driver.

CHAPTER ONE

A year later—San Antonia

'ARE YOU SURE you've got everything? Passports, tickets, keys to the flat?'

'Everything's under control—stop fretting,' Emily bade her friend cheerfully. 'You've got enough to worry about. The coach is here.'

Arrivals day was always hectic, she mused as she followed Laura out into the courtyard. The farmhouse at San Antonia had once been a quiet refuge for Laura's boyfriend and his crowd of artist friends. All that had changed when Nick had persuaded Laura to join him in Spain and she had opened up her cookery school. The business had been an instant success, catering for tourists eager to take lessons from an innovative chef who had earned her stars at a top London restaurant. Emily was pleased for Laura and glad she had been able to help out by organising the guests' living and sleeping facilities, but the time had come for her go back to England and take control of her life.

'I hope you'll manage,' she murmured as she joined her friend on the front step and watched the party alight from the coach. 'I could be away for a couple of months while the lawyers sort out the divorce.'

'From bitter experience, I'd better warn you it could take a lot longer than that,' Laura replied grimly. 'Mine took over a year to finalise and cost me a small fortune.'

'I'm not anticipating any problems,' Emily said with a shrug. 'Luc will be as pleased as me to see the end of our marriage.' Especially if the recent photo in one of the British tabloids was anything to go by, she thought bleakly. Seeing his dark, handsome features again had momentarily caused her heart to stop beating. She had been shocked to discover the effect he still had on her, even after more than a year apart, but it had been the sight of his companion, the stunningly beautiful Robyn Blake, that had been the catalyst for her decision to bring a legal end to their farcical marriage.

It was time to put the past behind her, she thought resolutely. She had a baby, a burgeoning new business of her own and the freedom to live her life the way she chose. She enjoyed her independence, she reminded herself fiercely. She had fought hard to rebuild her self-respect and it was time to sever the legal ties that bound her to Jean-Luc Vaillon.

'How do you think you'll feel about seeing your husband again?' Laura asked.

'With any luck, I won't have to. I don't want anything from him, certainly not money,' Emily added fiercely.

'You're entitled to demand that he make proper provision for Jean-Claude,' Laura pointed out. 'Luc is his father after all, and it won't hurt him to dip into the Vaillon millions.'

'No!' Emily instantly refuted the suggestion. 'I'm responsible for my son and I'll provide for him. Luc never wanted a child. Jean-Claude's conception was an accident and I refuse to use him as leverage for financial gain. I'll manage,' she assured her friend brightly when Laura frowned in concern, 'but I won't take anything from Luc.'

In theory it all seemed so simple. She would make contact with Luc through a third party, and if he expressed any interest in seeing his son, the lawyers could thrash out the access arrangements along with the divorce. She wasn't expecting any complications but as she glanced over to where Jean-Claude was sleeping in his pushchair, shaded from the sun by a parasol, she was filled with a sense of foreboding. Nothing about Jean-Luc Vaillon was simple. He was a man of secrets and despite the fact that they had been married for two years, she didn't really know him at all.

'Someone's arrived in style.' Laura's voice broke into her thoughts and she glanced across the courtyard at the sleek black limousine that had swung in behind the coach. 'I hope they appreciate that this is a working holiday. I won't have time to run around after some spoilt millionaire's wife who can't boil an egg. The coach driver is quite happy to take you to the airport,' she added as she stepped forward to greet her guests. 'He's finished unloading now so you can give him your luggage before you have to disturb Jean-Claude.' She gave Emily a brief kiss on the cheek. 'Take care. We'll celebrate your new life as a single woman when you come back.'

A quick glance at the buggy revealed that Jean-Claude was still sleeping soundly and Emily decided to leave him for a few more minutes while she loaded her cases.

'How are you, Enzo?' she greeted the coach driver, who regularly made the journey between San Antonia and the airport.

'*Hola, Señora,* you're looking pretty today.'

Conversation about Enzo's huge extended family took another five minutes and when Emily looked back at the pushchair, it was empty. Laura must have taken Jean-Claude into the farmhouse, she thought, a prickle of unease threading along her spine. Something made her turn her head towards the car parked at the further end of the courtyard.

For a few seconds she thought it must be a trick of the light, a mirage brought on by the heat of the midday sun, but when she blinked she realised he was no illusion. Handsome was hardly an adequate description of him, she acknowledged numbly. This man was awesome, the power of his broad shoulders beneath his superbly tailored jacket so formidable that a trembling started deep inside her.

The air in the courtyard was still and sultry but she could not suppress a shiver as her eyes travelled up to the visitor's face and locked with his cold, grey stare. His eyes were hooded, hiding his expression, but she was struck by the hardness that emanated from him, the air of arrogance, of ruthlessness and sheer power, and she gave a cry as the world spun.

'Luc!'

Confusion made her close her eyes, as if by doing so she could rid herself of the unwelcome vision, but when she opened them again he was still there, larger than life, taller and more imposing than anyone she had ever met and her hands flew to cover her mouth, forcing back her cry.

'What are you doing here? What do you want?' she demanded tremulously, shock almost robbing her of her voice. He smiled, his mouth stretching to reveal his teeth so that she was reminded of a wolf preparing to devour its prey.

'I've already got what I came for, *chérie,*' he taunted softly, and she stared at him in confusion. 'It's up to you whether you choose to join us.'

'Us?' Emily parroted, her brain moving as sluggishly as

treacle. 'I don't understand.' She felt breathless and disorientated as he towered over her. Her heart was pounding and it took every ounce of her courage to lift her eyes to his face. If anything he was even more devastatingly good-looking than she remembered, leaner and harder than the man who regularly haunted her dreams. Looking at him caused a peculiar feeling inside, like a knife being thrust between her ribs, and she quickly tore her eyes away, blinking under the brilliant glare of the sun.

Luc's arrival at the farmhouse was so unexpected she didn't know what to do, what to say. 'How did you find me?' she croaked at last, and his expression hardened.

'You wrote to your solicitor, requesting that he start divorce proceedings,' he reminded her coolly. 'I must commend him for the speed with which he contacted my legal firm to set the wheels in motion.'

'Mr Carmichael has taken care of the Dyer family's legal matters for years,' Emily faltered. 'I specifically asked him to withhold my whereabouts and I don't believe he would have willingly handed you that information.'

'No, but his very pretty junior secretary proved much more amenable,' he murmured silkily. 'The evenings spent wining and dining her proved highly profitable—in more ways than one,' he added dulcetly, and the sudden gleam in his eyes sickened her.

'I really don't want to know the details of your grubby love life,' she snapped, hurt coursing through her, 'although from past experience I imagine *love* plays very little part in it. But I still don't understand why you're here,' she continued stonily, refusing to acknowledge that the familiar tang of the aftershave he favoured had evoked a host of memories she wished had remained buried. 'Presumably you read my letter explaining to Mr Carmichael that I would be returning to England to sort out the divorce. Why didn't you just wait for me?'

Luc inhaled sharply, his nostrils flaring as he sought to control the anger that surged through him. 'I have spent almost a year longing to see my child,' he ground out savagely, his eyes as cold and hard as slate, and Emily shivered as she realised the full extent of his fury. 'Did you really expect me to wait passively, hoping you would show up? Do you have any idea what it felt like to learn from a letter you'd sent your solicitor that I had fathered a son? *Sacré bleu!*' he ground out, his jaw rigid with tension. 'You were happy to inform Monsieur Carmichael, but you didn't even have the decency to tell me my son had been born, and for that I can never forgive you.'

'Why should I have done?' Emily defended herself, genuinely puzzled by his anger. 'Why would I have rushed to tell you I'd given birth to our child when you were so vehemently opposed to his conception? You made it clear that you didn't want either of us, Luc, so how can you blame me for wanting to bring Jean-Claude up among people who care for him?'

'If you think I will allow my child to spend his formative years in a hippy commune you are even more delusional that I thought,' he snarled furiously. 'I have lost the first precious months of my son's life and I hold you and your half-baked theories about my supposed affair with my personal assistant completely to blame. Jealousy is not an attractive emotion, *chérie,*' he said, his eyes raking over her trembling form disparagingly. 'You allowed your childish craving for attention to colour your judgement but the one to suffer most is our son. You had no right to deny him a relationship with me, and from now on he will know exactly who his father is,' he told her forcefully, his gaze brimful of bitterness that corroded her soul.

'I would never prevent you from seeing Jean-Claude, if that's what you want,' she muttered as she tried to come to terms with the astounding realisation that Luc seemed to want his son after all. Perhaps it had only been the sight of her pregnant body that had filled him with revulsion, she thought bitterly. 'I assumed you would want nothing to do with him but I'm prepared to be reasonable about access arrangements if you've really lost your aversion to fatherhood.'

'How very generous of you.' Luc's voice dripped with sarcasm and she flushed. He'd always had the knack of making her feel two feet high and once she would have backed down at the slightest hint of confrontation. Now she lifted her chin and stared at him, cursing her body's involuntary reaction to him. How could he still have such an effect on her after everything he'd put her through, the humiliation he'd heaped on her?

She'd been overwhelmed from the first moment she'd set eyes on him, she acknowledged grimly. There was something about his face, the sharp cheekbones and very slightly hooked nose, that gave him the appearance of a hawk, his eyes gleaming from beneath heavy black brows, watchful and calculating. It was hard to believe that those eyes had once softened to the colour of woodsmoke, that the cruel line of his mouth had moulded into a sensual curve as he had explored her lips with a degree of passion and tenderness that had left her weak with longing.

She bit back a gasp as a curious pain uncoiled in the pit of her stomach, self-disgust swamping her as her imagination ran riot. What was desire doing, rearing its ugly head at a time like this, when Luc was studying her with insolent appraisal as if she was something unpleasant that had crawled out from beneath a stone? Swiftly she crossed her arms over her chest to hide her body's blatant betrayal, sickness flooding through her when his gaze settled on her breasts and she saw his lip curl in sardonic amusement.

'But, then, in certain areas you were always very generous, weren't you, Emily?' he drawled. 'Especially in bed.'

'Go to hell,' she snapped, tears of mortification stinging her eyelids. How dared he look at her like that, as if she was some cheap tart and he was considering sampling her wares? 'I'm surprised you even remember. It's a long time since you chose to share my bed but, then, you didn't need to did you, Luc? You were busy elsewhere.' She broke off abruptly, twin spots of colour staining her cheeks. Now was not the time to reveal the depths of the clawing jealousy she'd experienced on those long, lonely nights when she'd waited in vain for him to come home.

'As soon as I arrive in London, I'll have my lawyers contact yours to arrange suitable access to Jean-Claude,' she told him briskly as she looked towards the farmhouse. No doubt Laura was struggling to give her guests a guided tour of the kitchens with Jean-Claude clamped to her hip. The sooner she held her son in her arms the happier she would be, she decided after risking another peep at Luc's inscrutable face. 'If you'll excuse me, I need to go and find him,' she murmured awkwardly. She supposed she should invite Luc into the farmhouse to meet his son and her conscience prickled uncomfortably as he continued to stare down at her with those laser-beam eyes that she was sure could read her mind.

She didn't want to take him inside, she acknowledged as a faint edge of apprehension gripped her once more. San

Antonia was her territory, and for some reason she would prefer Luc's first meeting with his son to take place on the neutral ground of her solicitor's office. Time was getting on, she realised with a glance at her watch. The coach driver was looking impatient and if she wasn't careful she would miss her flight.

'Are you in the habit of losing my son?' Luc enquired, his brows raised sardonically, and she flushed.

'Of course not. I haven't lost him, just mislaid him,' she added, her vain attempt to lighten the situation, receiving no flicker of response from him. 'So, I'll see you in London.' She needed to walk away from him but it seemed as if her feet were trapped in quicksand and she couldn't move as her eyes greedily absorbed every detail of his beloved face. Not that she loved him any more, her mind hastily pointed out, but he possessed a magnetism that even now was wrapping itself around her, making coherent thought impossible.

'As you wish.' The curtness of Luc's tone broke the spell and she became aware of his sudden impatience as he flicked back the sleeve of his jacket to read his watch. The brief glimpse of his tanned wrist, dusted with a sprinkling of fine black hairs, caused her tummy to lurch and she inhaled sharply. 'We need to make a move anyway.'

His words puzzled her and she gave a harsh laugh. 'Let me guess. Robyn is waiting in the car for you. I can't fault her dedication to duty,' she said sarcastically.

He was already walking away from her and paused briefly to glance over his shoulder. '*Oui,* Robyn's behaviour and attitude are exemplary,' he replied in a tone that clearly indicated her own failing in both departments. 'But she is not with me this time. Jean-Claude is in the car and, no doubt, growing restless. *Au revoir, chérie.*'

Incredibly he had already dipped his head prior to sliding into the car and her feet suddenly grew wings. 'Luc! Wait, what do you mean, he's in the car? Jean-Claude is in the house with Laura—isn't he?' she finished uncertainly, and the blandness of his expression only served to increase her fear.

'I took the liberty of stowing my son safely in the car while your attention was...' He paused fractionally. 'Elsewhere. Tell me, *chérie,* are you always so careless about leaving him unattended and in the full glare of the sun?'

'He was shaded by the parasol,' Emily defended herself fiercely, 'and I did not leave him unattended. He was asleep and I was...' She was going to explain how she had taken advantage of Jean-Claude's brief nap to load her luggage onto the coach, but the scathing disgust in Luc's eyes made her want to crawl away.

'You were too busy to watch over him. Anyone could have taken him.' He pushed home the point by glancing into the car and she flushed. It was true that her attention had been focused on the trip back to London, but she had regularly checked on the baby and, besides, the farmhouse was miles from anywhere. A person would have to have been extremely determined, not to mention devious, to snatch him and unfortunately the description fitted Jean-Luc Vaillon to the letter.

She had reached the car and her shocked glance revealed that Jean-Claude was indeed inside, strapped into a baby seat and happily absorbed playing with the brightly coloured toys in front of him. 'But you can't just take him,' she faltered, her shock giving way to stark fury. 'How dare you try to take him from me? I'm his mother.' She rounded on him, her voice bristling with outrage as her fingers fumbled with the door-handle.

Instantly his hand closed over hers, his grip bruising as he surveyed her steadily from beneath his ridiculously long, black lashes. 'And I am his father, yet you thought nothing of keeping him from me. You deliberately hid yourself away and if it hadn't been for your greed, it's possible that I still wouldn't have found you or, more importantly, my son.'

'My greed?' Emily echoed faintly.

'I assume you were banking on a hefty divorce settlement to keep you in the manner to which you've become accustomed,' he mocked, his disdainful glance taking in the rambling farmhouse and various outbuildings, 'although I'm not sure why you need money in this God-forsaken spot. Perhaps you want it for other reasons than providing a secure environment for Jean-Claude?'

'Such as?' She glared at him, one hand on her hip while the other was still trapped beneath his.

'Drugs?' he suggested with a nonchalant shrug that belied the gleam of anger in his eyes. 'Who knows what goes on inside your hippy commune? All I care is that it is not a suitable place to bring up a small child, certainly not my child.'

'Because, of course, you are such a caring parent.' She could hardly speak as her anger choked her. 'San Antonia is not some sort of drugs den. It's a thriving community where everyone works together and where my friend Laura runs a cookery school for middle-aged ladies. The only drugs you'll find here are for rheumatism or the menopause!'

'I have never been given the opportunity to prove my worth as a parent,' Luc snapped, 'but that's about to change. My son is coming with me.'

'The hell he is!' From the corner of her eye Emily saw the coach driver lean out of his window.

'*Señorita,* we have to go.'

'Yes, I won't be a minute.' She tried to open the car door but Luc's hand tightened around her fingers until she was sure they would break. 'For God's sake, Luc!' Tears brought on through a mixture of pain and fear filled her eyes. 'You can't have him.'

'On the contrary, *chérie,* I already have him. It's up to you whether you come, too. Personally speaking, you can rot in hell,' he told her savagely. 'I would enjoy watching you burn in the eternal flames, but for his sake I suggest you get in the car.' Abruptly he released the catch and opened the door while she stared wildly around the courtyard, searching for someone to help her.

'There's no way I'd allow you to take him without me,' she vowed fiercely, and then gave a despairing cry as the coach began to move. 'My luggage is on the coach. Enzo, wait!'

Enzo must have caught sight of her frantic waving in his mirror and braked, but it took Emily precious minutes to drag her cases from the luggage compartment, and when she looked round, the limousine was already rolling forward.

'You bastard, you knew I was coming,' she sobbed as she yanked open the rear door and threw her cases into the footwell while Luc made no attempt to ask his chauffeur to halt. She was panting as she scrambled into the car and pulled the door shut after her. 'I've a good mind to have you charged with kidnap,' she snapped, and his sardonic smile told her he was as aware as she that she stood no chance of carrying out her threat. The trap was sprung. She was entirely at his mercy, she realised and trepidation filled her as, with a barely discernible snick, the door lock was activated.

'Not kidnap,' he murmured coolly as his gaze settled on her flushed face, 'I prefer repossession. And I promise you, *chérie*, this time you will not escape!'

CHAPTER TWO

THE ATMOSPHERE INSIDE the car crackled with antagonism. Jean-Claude suddenly lost interest in his toys, stared unblinkingly at Luc and then back at Emily, his bottom lip wobbling.

'It's all right, Mama's here. No one's going to hurt you,' she reassured him softly, stroking his cheek, and he turned his enormous, velvet grey eyes on her, his tears drying as his face broke into a smile that revealed his one solitary tooth. Luc was sitting on the other side of the baby seat and he stiffened at her words, outrage and bitter, corrosive anger filling him.

'Of course I'm not going to hurt him,' he snarled, aware of the necessity of keeping his voice low so that he did not frighten Jean-Claude. 'What kind of barbarian do you think I am to suggest I would hurt my own son?'

'You don't want to know my opinion of you,' Emily returned, her smile solely for Jean-Claude's benefit, belying the venom in her voice. 'You tried to drive off without me. Don't you think that wrenching a young baby from his mother's arms would hurt him?'

'Don't be so dramatic,' Luc snapped impatiently. 'You weren't even with him. You'd abandoned him. What kind of mother does that make you?'

'A damn good one, and I did not abandon him.' Emily ran a shaky hand over her face as reaction set in. 'He's eleven months old, for heaven's sake. How do you think he would cope without me? He needs me.'

Luc surveyed her silently, his eyes raking disparagingly over her slender figure and she cringed, wishing she'd worn anything but her bright orange gypsy skirt and yellow strap top. With her hair caught up in a ponytail secured with a livid yellow band and the long, beaded earrings and necklace that one of the artists had made for her, she looked funky and modern, a complete antithesis of the sophisticated, elegant women Luc admired. Women like his PA Robyn Blake.

'You're not as indispensable as you like to think,' he said icily. 'He'd soon forget you and instead of a mother he will have a father. However,' he continued, ignoring her fearful gasp, 'I accept that it is in Jean-Claude's best interests that you play a part in his life, for now at least.'

'Meaning what exactly?'

'Meaning that the situation is likely to change as he grows older but at the moment he is a baby and naturally depends on you. It is for that reason alone that I have decided to take you back,' he informed her in his cold, clipped tones, and Emily's eyes grew to the size of saucers.

'Well, pardon me for not jumping for joy, but I don't want to be taken back. I'm perfectly content with my life the way it is—without you in it. In fact,' she stressed, 'I've never been happier.' As she spoke she made the mistake of looking at him and her face flamed as she felt her body's involuntary reaction to his seductive charm. She didn't want to feel like this. She didn't want to be pierced by this overwhelming, almost obsessive sexual attraction, and the worst of it was, he was aware of his power over her.

'I'm sure I can come up with a few ideas to keep you content,' he drawled with an arrogant smile that made her want to scream or hit him, or both. 'I don't remember having any problems satisfying you when we were first married. In fact, *chérie,* after a night in my bed, you used to remind me of a cat who'd gorged on cream.'

The last thing she needed was to be reminded of her total and utter weakness where he was concerned. One look from those flashing grey eyes and she had been putty in his hands, her body desperate to experience the ecstasy of his full possession. She had been little better than a sex slave, she thought disgustedly, and he had exerted his power over her ruthlessly, subjugating her to his will with shameful ease.

Luc had to be playing a cruel game with her, she thought desperately. His insinuation that he knew he could keep her happy by sleeping with her was his despicable way of reminding her of her vulnerability where he was concerned. But she had changed during the year they had spent apart. She had grown up and taken charge of her emotions. With his incredible looks and raw, sexual magnetism, it wasn't surprising that he had once had such a strong hold over her but she had broken free of his spell and she refused to be bewitched again.

Jean-Claude was watching her and the beauty of his smile tore at her heart. He was innocently unaware of the bitterness that existed between his parents, a bitterness that would only fester if they were forced together again. At the moment he was just a baby, but as he grew older he would detect the signs that his parents detested one another and would surely be damaged by their antagonism.

'This is ridiculous,' she whispered huskily. 'For our son's sake, can't we call a truce and aim for an amicable divorce instead of fighting over him? Surely the most important thing is to give Jean-Claude the best upbringing we can?'

'I agree,' Luc replied, his gaze clashing with hers, 'which is why there will be no divorce. Our son deserves to be brought up by two parents who love him, even if they do not love each other,' he continued, ignoring Emily's shocked gasp. 'You will remain my wife, *chérie,* for better or worse. And make no mistake,' he warned her in a tone that gave some indication of his determination, 'it will be a proper marriage, in every sense of the word.'

'You can't really expect me to…to sleep with you,' Emily spluttered, outrage rendering her temporarily speechless as the full meaning of his words sank in.

'Why not? Our marriage may have had its problems, but the sex was always good. You were the most responsive lover I've ever known,' he told her, and she died a little at the way he could discuss something that had been so precious to her with such clinical detachment.

'Well, you've known a lot so I'll take your word for it but I'm afraid it's not an experience I want to repeat.'

'Is that so, *ma petite?*' The sudden amusement in his voice fuelled her anger and she curled her fingers into fists so that her nails bit into her palms. 'Time will tell, although not too much time, I hope. Patience isn't one of my finer virtues.'

'I'd rather kill myself than bear your touch again,' she snapped with a shudder as she contemplated the certain humiliation that would follow if she ever lowered her guard against him. He inhaled sharply, a nerve jumping in his cheek as he stared at her.

'Don't joke about such things, especially as we both know that you're lying,' he ground out, and she jerked her head round, startled by the bitterness in his eyes. 'You might have wrapped that cloak of virginal shyness around you like a nun's habit but you were a whore in the bedroom. Not that I'm complaining,' he added silkily when she turned her stunned, pain-filled eyes on him. 'I may be willing to put up with your presence in my life for Jean-Claude's sake, but I think I'm entitled to some compensations!'

He swung away to stare out of the window and in the ragged silence that followed his shocking statement she could only stare at his harsh profile. He really hated her, she realised as a combination of pain and panic washed over her. During the brief months they'd spent together after their marriage, she'd glimpsed his ruthless streak in his business dealings. Beneath his charismatic charm lurked a merciless disregard for anyone who dared cross him, and despite his insistence that their marriage would continue, he viewed her as the enemy. For a moment she quailed but from somewhere her pride came to the rescue and she lifted her chin.

'You don't really want me back, any more than you want to play happy families with Jean-Claude. I intend to seek a divorce, Luc, and I'll fight you tooth and nail for my baby. You never wanted him and I can prove that while I was pregnant you were too busy sleeping with your bloody secretary to give a damn about your unborn child or me. This has nothing to do with wanting Jean-Claude, has it?' She pressed on, ignoring the ominous tightening of his jaw that gave some indication of his fury. 'This is about your obsession to win, the need to exert your power. You didn't want me and perhaps when you were good and ready you'd have divorced me, but you can't bear the fact that I was the one to walk away. I defied you and now you want to punish me by claiming the child you never even wanted to be born.'

'Enough!' His voice stung like the crack of a whip as he

jerked his head round to face her and Emily visibly flinched, although she refused to drop her gaze. Once she had been in awe of him, her painful lack of self-confidence no match for his brilliant mind and acerbic wit, but she had Jean-Claude to fight for now and she glared across the car, determined not be cowed. '*Mon Dieu!* You have developed the tongue of a viper. I am trying very hard to be fair, which is more than you deserve when you never once gave me the same considera-tion. You stole my son, and like a thief in the night you hid him from me. Let me set something straight once and for all Emily,' he growled. 'I always wanted our child. I longed to hold our baby in my arms, but for all these months you denied me even the knowledge of his existence. Now, finally, I have found him and nothing in this world will ever make me let him go. If you insist on filing for divorce I can't stop you, but I will fight you for Jean-Claude with all the means at my disposal, and financially those means are considerable. If you want there to be war between us rather than peace, go ahead, but I hope you have the stomach for it because it is a war I *will* win.'

The car was speeding along the road, the locked doors pre-venting her escape even if it had been possible to jump out. The plush leather upholstery, the uniformed chauffeur and the discreet but well-stocked bar all indicated a level of wealth that would render any legal fight between them a waste of time. Luc could afford the best lawyers and if he chose to seek custody of Jean-Claude she would stand no chance against him. For the moment at least, she was out of options. Luc had won as usual and she seethed silently. 'I hate you,' she spat at him, and he shrugged indifferently.

'I'm devastated, *chérie,* but I won't force you to endure my company. If you really can't make Jean-Claude and what's best for him your priority, then you'd better get out now. Say the word and I'll ask my driver to stop and drop you off.'

Emily glanced out at the barren landscape, which was as dry and unforgiving as a desert. The empty road snaked past jutting boulders and huge, spiteful cacti, and once again fear gripped her. 'You surely wouldn't abandon us out here, miles from anywhere?' she whispered and Luc gave her a chilling smile.

'Of course not. I've told you, from now on Jean-Claude stays with me. But you are free to go wherever and whenever you like, *mon amour.*'

'Don't call me that,' she said sharply, her body clenching in rejection of the careless endearment that even now had the power to make her long for the moon. She had never been his love. 'Your cruelty is beyond belief,' she whispered, and he gave a harsh laugh.

'That you can accuse *me* of cruelty when you stole my son is also beyond belief but believe this, Emily, I do not forgive easily, and I will never forget.'

The barely concealed bitterness in his voice shook her and she took a deep breath as she concentrated on the scenery flashing past. Slowly her panic faded slightly as she envisaged the bustling airport. Presumably Luc was intending to fly back to England, but he would hardly be able to frogmarch her and Jean-Claude aboard a plane. Hopefully, if she kept her wits, there would be an opportunity to snatch back her son and slip away.

She forced herself to relax and bide her time, but in the tense silence her eyes turned involuntarily towards the man whose presence dominated the car. It wasn't fair that he was so gorgeous, she thought bleakly, feeling a knife skewer her heart as she studied his stern profile. His incredible bone structure could have been fashioned from marble by one of the Old Masters. His olive-gold skin stretched taut over the hard planes of his face. Despite the fact that he was in his late thirties, there was no hint of silver in his thick black hair, and she closed her eyes on a wave of pain as she remembered the feel of it against her fingers when she had pulled his head down to hers. His mouth was to die for and he had delighted in teasing every inch of her body with it, his tongue a wicked instrument of torturous pleasure during their long hours of loving that had left her utterly satiated.

That had been a long time ago, she hastily reminded herself. In those first heady weeks of their marriage when she'd almost convinced herself she had done the right thing by marrying the enigmatic Frenchman and that he might one day even grow to love her as she loved him.

The illusion had been quickly shattered. They had spent the weekend after their wedding in Paris, too absorbed in their mutual passion for each other to do much sightseeing. On their arrival back in London, Luc had swept her into his arms as the lift carried them up to his penthouse flat, but instead of carrying her straight to the bedroom, he had hesitated in the doorway as the most beautiful woman Emily had ever seen moved forward to greet them.

Robyn Blake, once a world-famous model, was Luc's sister-in-law as well as his personal assistant. She was exquisite, there was no other word to describe her, and Emily had immediately felt young and gauche, aware that her chain-store dress had been no match for Robyn's designer outfit.

At first she had been taken in by Robyn's apparent friendliness. Having spent her childhood in the shadow of her sisters, she was plagued by a crushing lack of self-confidence and had followed Robyn around like a puppy desperate to please its master. She had sought the older woman's advice on everything from clothes and make-up to the problems that were emerging in her marriage, and it had taken her a long time to realise that Robyn was the cause of many of those problems.

She could not lay all the blame at Robyn's door, she admitted miserably. Her own insecurity and lack of self-belief hadn't helped any more than the growing realisation that Jean-Luc Vaillon was incapable of loving anyone. He had treated her suspicions about the true nature of his relationship with his PA with scathing dismissal. It was time she grew up instead of behaving like a silly child, he'd told her, but in her heart she accepted that he had never felt more than a faint affection for her and now she had proof that his reasons for making her his wife had been far more prosaic than love.

With a sigh she turned to find Luc watching Jean-Claude. He seemed utterly absorbed, as though he could not drag his gaze from his son, but he must have felt her scrutiny and she blushed as he lifted his head and subjected her to a hard stare. Pride dictated that she should turn away but she was trapped by the brooding sensuality that emanated from him, her eyes focused on his mouth, remembering the taste of him, the feel of his lips on hers. Suddenly she was too hot. The air inside the car seemed stifling despite the air-conditioning, and tiny beads of sweat formed above her top lip. She wanted to wipe them away but her hands were trembling and she shoved them into her lap, her tongue darting out to capture the salty pearls on its tip.

Luc's eyes narrowed as he watched the nervous foray of her tongue and she knew with humiliating certainty that he was aware of her thoughts. What was the matter with her? she asked herself impatiently. He despised her, his contempt clearly visible in the cool grey gaze that speared her. He only tolerated her presence for the sake of his son so why was she consumed with this wild longing to feel his mouth on hers? She hated him, her mind totally rejected his ruthless power, but it seemed that her body had a will of its own and it recognised its master.

With a barely suppressed gasp she tore her gaze from his, biting down hard on her lip until she tasted blood. Luc was a cheat and a liar and he had broken her heart. For the sake of her self-preservation it was crucial that she remembered that fact.

'Don't look at me like that,' she demanded, seeking refuge in her anger. 'You lost the right to look at me like you own me when you increased your *personal* assistant's duties.'

'You're still blinded by your ridiculous insecurities, I see,' Luc murmured coolly, and her cheeks flooded with colour as his jibe hit home. She had always been so unsure of herself, especially where he was concerned, and she hated the fact that he had been aware of her vulnerability.

With her head turned determinedly away from him, Luc was left with the view of Emily's taut shoulders and his eyes rested on the curve of her cheek and one small, pink ear, her long, dangly earring emphasising the slender column of her neck. She looked heartbreakingly young with her glorious chestnut hair caught up on top of her head. A few tendrils had escaped to curl around her cheek and he fought the urge to reach across and brush them back behind her ear, to cup her chin in his hand and turn her face to his.

What was he thinking? he berated himself furiously. This woman, *his wife,* had walked out on him without a backward glance. Not only that, but she had disappeared so conclusively that gossip and speculation among London's society had been rife. He had been terrified for her safety, not knowing if she was alive or dead, but for all those long months she had been living quite comfortable in her Spanish hide-away.

Her accusation that he hadn't wanted their child was ridiculous. His longing for their baby had shaken him with its intensity, but alongside hope had been fear. His secret terror that history would repeat itself had made him appear distant and his perceived disinterest had cost him dear.

He inhaled sharply and forced himself to drop his gaze to the baby who was sitting quietly in his child seat. Jean-Claude, his son. It still seemed incredible that this beautiful, wide-eyed baby was his own flesh and blood, yet there was no mistaking the likeness between them and his heart clenched in primitive recognition. Wonderingly he touched the baby's satiny curls, which were as black as his own hair, and when Jean-Claude lifted his long lashes to survey him solemnly with huge, grey eyes, it was like looking into a mirror. His son, the child he'd feared he would never see. He loved him instantly, a huge wave of adoration sweeping through him, and he vowed that nothing would ever separate him from his child again.

'He looks like you,' Emily said grudgingly as she watched Jean-Claude smile at his father. From the moment her son had first opened his eyes and focused on her, she'd been taken aback by his likeness to Luc. It was as if fate itself was on Luc's side, determined that he would not be forgotten, but seeing them together brought home to her that her baby was all Vaillon, truly his father's son.

Jean-Claude regarded the stranger solemnly. At almost a year old, he knew his own mind, knew whom he liked and whom he didn't, and Emily felt a sharp stab of jealousy when he stretched out his chubby arms to Luc. Would all Vaillon men betray her? she wondered bitterly. And then dismissed the shabby thought. She wanted Jean-Claude to have a good relationship with his father and incredibly it now seemed that Luc shared that desire. Perhaps, once he had calmed down, she could broach the idea of divorce once more. She was certain he did not really want her as his wife and if she assured him of her willingness to share custody of Jean-Claude, their parting could at least be amicable.

'Jean-Claude and I are booked on an evening flight to London,' she murmured. 'It seems silly to waste the tickets but I'll meet you as soon as possible, tomorrow if you insist,' she added when Luc made no reply and simply surveyed her with his cool grey stare.

'I'm not taking him to London,' he replied at last, and she stared at him in confusion.

'Then where are you going?' She had hated Luc's Chelsea penthouse, which had all the appeal of a dentist's waiting room and had never felt like her home, but Luc had seemed perfectly at ease there and she assumed it was still his London base.

'To France, of course. Jean-Claude is a Vaillon, my son and heir. Naturally he will be brought up in my homeland,' he informed her, his brows raised in surprise that there could be any doubt.

'Naturally,' Emily snapped sarcastically, 'but what about my homeland? Hasn't it occurred to you that I'd like to bring him up in England?

'But you weren't, were you?' he pointed out silkily. 'For some peculiar reason you decided that an artists' commune in the middle of the Spanish wilderness was the best place for our son to live. But no longer. From now on Jean-Claude will enjoy all the benefits of his heritage at my château in the

Loire Valley. The Vaillons are an old French family. Surely you would not want to deprive him of his birthright?'

'I didn't even know you owned a château. Something else you failed to mention. But what of Jean-Claude's British heritage?' Emily argued, panic assailing her once more at Luc's resolute expression. 'The Dyers are an old family, too. Heston Grange was their ancestral seat for over four hundred years, until you bought it,' she finished bleakly. 'Tell me,' she demanded with a hollow laugh, 'did you know from the beginning that my parents hoped you would marry one of their daughters so that the Dyers would retain some link with the family's heritage? Did they offer you Heston at a fraction of its value as long as you agreed to marry one of us? And if that's true, Luc, why on earth did you pick me? I was the plain one, the drab Dyer, more at home with horses than people. My sisters are beautiful, clever and sophisticated, any one of them would have made you a far more suitable wife, but I suppose you thought I would be the easiest to manipulate, the one least likely to make a fuss when you resumed your relationship with your mistress.'

At twenty she had been shy and severely lacking in confidence, unable to disguise her massive crush on the handsome, enigmatic Frenchman who had turned all their lives upside down, but to him she must have seemed a pushover. She had been a pawn in a far more serious game.

'You always did seriously undervalue yourself,' Luc murmured dryly, as his eyes skimmed her flushed face and huge navy blue eyes. 'I admit there were a number of reasons why you were suitable...'

'All to do with money and prestige, and none to do with love,' Emily finished for him. She didn't want to hear every cold, calculated detail of why he had decided to marry her.

She already knew it was because her parents had offered him Heston Grange at a massively reduced price if he married one of the Dyer daughters, thereby retaining the family's link with their heritage. It was archaic, she thought bitterly. She felt like a brood mare, sold off with a suitable dowry, but Luc hadn't even wanted her for her childbearing ability. He hadn't wanted children at all, which made his sudden determination to gain custody of their son all the more shocking.

'Jean-Claude is a Vaillon,' Luc repeated stubbornly, 'and from now on the Château Montiard will be his home, not some filthy dump in the middle of nowhere.'

'San Antonia is not filthy. The farmhouse is beautiful and Jean-Claude loved it there.'

'Really.' Luc's brows rose as he murmured sardonically. 'He must be a child prodigy to express his opinion when he's not even a year old. Tell me, *chérie,* what would you have done if he'd been taken ill? The nearest hospital is miles away. For someone who expresses such maternal devotion, you seem to have little regard for his well-being.'

'While you, of course, are an expert on child care,' Emily snapped furiously. 'Jean-Claude was perfectly well cared for, but it's not easy being a single mother and I was grateful for the help of the other members of the commune.'

'You were a single mother by choice,' he pointed out hardily, 'but you never gave Jean-Claude a choice. You forced him to live his life with only one parent and you denied me a relationship with my own son. Now it's your turn to suffer,' he told her darkly, and she shivered at the contempt in his gaze.

'For heaven's sake, can't we be adult about this?' she cried despairingly and he gave a harsh laugh.

'It would be a first for you, *chérie,* that's for sure, but I'm afraid you've pushed me way beyond the boundaries of wanting to be reasonable. Now that I have my son I have no intention of ever letting him go, and there's not a damn thing you can do about it.'

The car was slowing and Emily glanced out of the window, frantically searching for the signs to the airport, but there were none. Instead they drove through the gates of what appeared to be a private airfield and sick fear gripped her. How could she have forgotten that Luc owned his own private jet? There was no bustling airport, no queues at the check-in desk where there might have been an opportunity to grab Jean-Claude and run. Luc's plane was ready and waiting on the runway. He had stated that he was prepared to take her to his château for their son's sake but he couldn't force her to resume the role of his wife, could he?

Suddenly her pride was an expendable commodity she would gladly sacrifice in return for her baby and she stared beseechingly at Luc as the car drew to a halt. 'Please, don't do this,' she begged huskily. 'I can't live without Jean-Claude but neither can I live with you. You must see that.'

'Surely, if you have any sense of fairness you must see that it is my turn to have him now,' Luc replied coldly. 'Jean-Claude is coming home with me, with or without you.'

'But you didn't want him!' she cried, her voice rising with frustration. 'From the moment you knew I was pregnant you made it clear that you had no interest in either of us. You slept in another room,' she reminded him huskily, 'when you bothered to come back to the flat at all. And you were completely uninvolved in my pregnancy. You didn't even show up at the hospital for my ultrasound scan.

'Do you have any idea how I felt that morning?' she demanded bitterly as a wave of memories hit her. 'The fact that you'd spent the night with Robyn was unforgivable but I still thought…hoped you cared enough about our child to want to see the first pictures of him. I sat in that waiting room alone surrounded by excited, happy couples, and I prayed you would come,' she whispered brokenly. Every time they called my name I allowed someone else to go in my place until there was no one left, just me on my own with a very sympathetic nurse who tried to make a joke about men being useless time-keepers.' She scrubbed her eyes furiously with the back of her hand, desperate that he didn't see her cry. 'But you hadn't mistaken the time, had you, Luc? You just didn't care about the baby or me, and that's why I left. I knew I'd outstayed my welcome.'

'That's not true,' he began, his face twisting with emotions she refused to try and decipher any more.

'It is true,' she cried angrily. 'I didn't need any more proof of your indifference. How can you blame me for questioning your motives now?' she finished brokenly.

Luc paused as he opened the door. She looked as young and innocent as on that first day when she had stared up at him and an arrow had pierced his heart. He wanted to hate her—indeed, there had been many times during the past year when he'd convinced himself that he despised her—but she was watching him with those expressive blue eyes. He glimpsed her vulnerability and something tugged at his heart.

He had never been any good at saying how he felt, he conceded, and his conscience prickled as he remembered how his unspoken fears had caused him to appear tense and uncommunicative. His childhood had left scars, a wariness of revealing his emotions. He hadn't forgotten her scan. *Dieu,* he would have given anything to be with her but Robyn had been distraught, he had been torn and by the time he had managed to phone and explain the situation, Emily had already left for the hospital. He had been too late but at that point he hadn't realised the extent of the damage his decision had cost him, and he had never been given the chance to make amends.

'Wait there while I see if they're ready for us,' he growled as he climbed out of the car. 'I have employed a nanny to take care of Jean-Claude. It might be better if he meets her before we get on the plane.'

'He doesn't need a nanny,' Emily pointed out sharply. 'I can look after him perfectly well on my own.'

'*Mon Dieu!* Do you have to argue about everything?' He was already striding across the tarmac and she watched him go, adrenalin coursing through her as she tapped on the car's glass partition to gain the attention of the chauffer. This was probably a hired car, she reasoned feverishly, and it was likely that the driver was Spanish.

'Drive on, please,' she requested in a confident tone that did not match the sick fear in the pit of her stomach. The months she'd spent in Spain meant that she was fairly fluent in the language and she smiled reassuringly at the driver. 'There's been a change of plan and Señor Vaillon wishes you to take me to the international airport.'

The chauffer was young and his dark eyes flashed with a boldness he made no effort to hide as he responded to her smile.

'*Sí, señora.*'

The car rolled forward and she took a sharp breath. 'As quickly as you can, *por favor.*' But it was too late. Luc must have moved faster than the speed of light and already he was wrenching the door open.

'You little bitch,' he swore at her savagely, his face contorted with fury. He yelled at the driver to cut the engine and swiftly released Jean-Claude's safety harness before lifting him into his arms. 'I was prepared to be fair, to treat you with a respect that you clearly don't deserve. But not any more,' he snarled as his fingers curled around her arm.

'Is everything all right, Monsieur Vaillon?' The woman at the bottom of the plane's steps looked calm and professional in her grey uniform. Presumable she was the nanny Luc had hired, Emily thought desperately as she struggled to break free of his bruising grip.

'Shall I take the baby?'

'*Merci.*' Luc transferred Jean-Claude into the woman's arms and immediately turned his attention back to Emily, his eyes dark and dispassionate as he watched a single tear roll down her face.

'You can't do this,' she whispered as he jerked her into his arms.

'Watch me,' he taunted, and before she realised his intentions his head obliterated the sunlight. It was not so much a kiss as a public branding, his lips hot and hard, forcing hers apart and uncaring if he evoked a response. Emily was so shocked that she simply leaned against his chest fearing that her legs would buckle beneath her. Her humiliation was complete when she was forced to cling to him for support. It was as quick as it was brutal and he released her with a savage imprecation while she stared up at him, her trembling fingers covering her mouth. For a few brief seconds she had been on fire for him, her body reacting instantaneously to his raw sexuality, and her cheeks burned with shame at the speculative gleam in his eyes. He knew the effect he had on her, knew that for those few seconds he had made her forget everything, even her son, and with that knowledge came power.

'Take your hands off me,' she demanded, her voice shaking with outrage, and he threw back his head and laughed.

'You're a good actress, I'll give you that. But you don't fool me, *ma chérie*. I know you too well and I have forgotten nothing. I remember vividly what pleases you,' he breathed in her ear and the warmth of his breath on her skin caused a trembling within her that had nothing to do with fear. 'Welcome back, my sweet wife,' he goaded softly as he put his hand in the small of her back and pushed her up the steps into the waiting jet.

CHAPTER THREE

WHAT THE *HELL* had he done?

Luc stared moodily at the glass on the tray in front of him and with a muttered oath snatched it up and downed its contents in one gulp, although he rarely drank alcohol in the middle of the day. Right now he needed something to anaesthetise the effect that Emily had on him—had always had on him, he admitted begrudgingly, although fortunately she seemed unaware that his emotions were veering dangerously out of control.

She was sitting away from him at the front of the plane, nursing Jean-Claude who had taken an instant dislike to his new surroundings and let his displeasure be known in no uncertain terms. The nanny he had employed, Liz Crawford, had an impressive record in child care, but she had been unable to pacify the baby, whose cries had only subsided once he was in his mother's arms.

'He needs me,' Emily had insisted, and watching them now, mother and son, Luc knew she was right. She was cradling Jean-Claude against her shoulder, rocking gently as she sang to him in her sweet, husky voice, and Luc felt a curious twisting in his gut as he recognised the familiar French lullaby that evoked memories of his own childhood.

He shouldn't have kissed her, he conceded grimly. He shouldn't have given in to the basic, almost primal need to hold her in his arms once more. He needed to be in control, to take things slowly and persuade her that coming back to him would be the best thing for all of them, not just the baby.

He had convinced himself that he had every right to hate her but from the moment he'd walked across the courtyard at San Antonia the battle being waged in his head had been lost. She had deprived him of the first year of his son's life, and when he'd received notice from her solicitor that she wanted a divorce he had been ready to commit murder. If she no longer wanted to be his wife, that was fine, he had assured himself, because he'd had enough of feeling a fool and he didn't want her back.

Brave words, but unfortunately, as soon as he'd set eyes on her he'd known he could not back them up. He still wanted her, heaven help him. She was in his blood and he'd known instantly that he couldn't let her go, but the flash of fear in her eyes when she first caught sight of him had shaken him. He had never been an ogre, had he? She had no reason to cower from him and as he stared at her it was confusion rather than anger that filled him. She had ripped his heart out, damn it, when his only crime had been to fear for her safety. He wanted her but he was determined to discover the truth about why she had left him before he could even begin to trust her again. It was nothing more than sexual attraction, he consoled himself. The fierce chemistry that had existed from the moment they'd first met still burned for both of them. He wasn't blind, he had seen the way she'd looked at him in the car, had known she felt the same primitive tug of awareness, and when he'd kissed her he had felt her response despite her efforts to hide it.

He set his glass back on the tray and resisted the urge to ask for another drink. He might tell himself that he had every right to despise Emily, but the unpalatable truth was that she had stolen his heart long before she had stolen his child. He resented the hold she had over him but seeing her again had forced him to accept that their lives were inextricably linked for ever.

Jean-Claude's sobs gradually subsided as he fell asleep and Emily reluctantly handed him over to the nanny, who took charge of him with an air of quiet authority. Not knowing what to do, unsure of her role, she glanced round and grimaced as Luc beckoned that she should join him.

'Why did you sing to him in French?' he demanded when she slid into the seat beside him, the expression in his eyes unfathomable as he studied her small, delicate face and the way the strap of her top had slid down to leave her shoulder bare.

'I hoped to bring him up to recognise both English and French,' Emily explained, her cheeks pink as she hastily re-adjusted the strap. 'One of the artists at San Antonia was French and she taught me some lullabies to sing to him.' She bit her lip at the unforgiving hardness of Luc's face.

'I honestly believed you didn't want him,' she said huskily, 'but I still hoped to give you a chance to meet him. I want Jean-Claude to know his father and I was going to tell my solicitor that I was happy for us to share custody.'

'Then why hide away in Spain?' he demanded impatiently and she sighed.

'I was ill after Jean-Claude was born. It was a difficult birth and it took me a while to recover. I was staying at my friend Laura's flat while she set up her cookery school at San

Antonia and she invited me to Spain to recuperate. I was so busy looking after a new baby and helping Laura and the time passed so quickly...'

'What do you mean by a difficult birth?' Luc growled. 'Are you saying there were problems?'

'It was a long labour, thirty-eight hours and he was a big baby. I lost a lot of blood,' Emily admitted, and Luc's face darkened as he fought to control the nausea that swept through him. He should have been there. She should have given him the opportunity to support her during her labour but he had driven her away. She was his wife, the woman he had sworn to protect, but once again, it seemed, he had failed in his duty.

'If you had stayed with me, you would have received the best medical care,' he muttered savagely, trying to disguise his pain. 'You needn't have suffered, yet out of spite, a ridiculous urge to hurt me, you put not just your life at risk but his, too.'

'Hurt you!' Emily stared at her husband with blank incomprehension in her eyes. 'When I mentioned the idea of starting a family you were adamant that you didn't want children. Jean-Claude's conception was a mistake—somehow the antibiotics I'd been prescribed interfered with the reliability of the Pill—but you refused to believe me. I remember how angry you were when I told you I was pregnant. It's not something a new bride is likely to forget,' she added painfully.

'*Sacré bleu!* It was our honeymoon,' Luc said explosively, 'and you did not tell me, *chérie,* you waited until we were on a remote island in the Indian Ocean before you collapsed. It was the emergency medic airlifted from the mainland who informed me of your condition.'

He could not repress a shudder as he relived the moment he had lifted her limp, lifeless body into his arms and had run up the beach, calling frantically for help. It was happening all over again his mind had drummed over and over, dismissing any semblance of calm in a tidal wave of terror. He had truly believed he had been about to lose her and it had been as devastating as the realisation of how deeply he cared. He had been unable to bear the thought of carrying on without her. He wasn't strong enough to survive such pain again, and even after it was made clear that she was in no danger, he had withdrawn into himself as a form of self-protection. He didn't want to love her. Love hurt.

'I hadn't known I was pregnant. It was as much of a shock to me as it was to you,' Emily muttered miserably, but with a savage oath, Luc swung away from her, flipped open his laptop and was instantly immersed in his work.

He obviously did not want to discuss the past, she thought darkly. Perhaps he felt guilty about the way he had treated her. She didn't know and she told herself that she didn't care. She knew from experience that he would resent any disturbance while he was working and she stared bleakly out of the window, wishing she found it as easy to dismiss him from her thoughts.

She must have been the only member of the Dyer household who had forgotten the dinner party planned to honour the potential saviour of Heston Grange, Emily recalled as memories of her first meeting with Luc filled her mind. Rushing in from the stables in her muddy jodhpurs, she had stumbled to a halt, her embarrassment excruciating when she'd viewed her elegant sisters and silently seething mother, but everything had faded to insignificance when she'd caught sight of Jean-Luc Vaillon for the first time.

The world really could tilt on its axis, she thought with a rueful smile, remembering the way she had literally grabbed hold of the back of a chair for support when he'd surveyed her with his cool grey stare. With his amazing facial bone structure and lean, hard body, he had been the sexiest man she had ever met and she had been unable to repress a shiver when he'd trapped her startled gaze with his, the gleam of amusement in those silvery depths warning her that he was aware of the effect he'd had on her.

Conscious of her mother's impatience, she fled upstairs to change into her serviceable navy-blue dress and spent the evening peeping at Luc from beneath her lashes, leaving her sisters to impress him with their sparkling conversation. The head of Vaillon Developments was irresistible with his suave good looks and seductive charm, but despite her sisters' frantic efforts to capture his attention, Emily glanced up several times during dinner to find him watching her. Embarrassment saw her quickly drop her gaze, but throughout the evening he continued to regard her with a mixture of amusement and another, indefinable emotion in his dark grey eyes.

'I have a feeling you are happier in the company of horses than humans,' he remarked a few days later, when he suddenly appeared in the stables. He had accepted her parents' suggestion to stay at Heston and discuss plans for its possible acquisition, but Emily was too shy to respond to his friendly charm and went out of her way to avoid him.

His husky French accent caused a delicious shiver to run all the way down to her toes, and she blushed and half hid her face against the mane of her darling Arab stallion, Kasim.

'I find horses are generally less complicated,' she agreed huskily, and his slow smile took her breath away. He remained chatting for several minutes, displaying an impressive knowledge of horsemanship, although she had been too tongue-tied to respond and afterwards had been furious with herself. She must have appeared a halfwit, but surprisingly he came again the next day, and the next, requesting that she ride out with him, and it was during those blissful excursions through the New Forest that she found herself falling in love with him.

What a fool she'd been, she now thought bitterly, to believe that the charismatic multimillionaire Frenchman would really be interested in a plain little nobody like her. Common sense should have warned her that he must have a hidden agenda, especially when he'd proposed to her so soon after they'd first met. She had ignored her doubts, swept away by his passionate kisses when he'd followed her into the stables and pulled her down into the hay. He'd overwhelmed her senses. She'd loved the way he'd made her feel, loved him and amazingly he'd seemed to want her, too.

Their wedding, in the magnificent grounds of Heston Grange, had been like a fairy-tale, a dream come true, and the dream had lasted for the whole of that first weekend when he had whisked her off to Paris. She had been a virgin on her wedding night, due only to his iron self-control. The memory of the way he had made love to her for the first time still brought tears to her eyes. He had been so tender, so gentle, treating her reverently as if she were made of the finest porcelain. Her untutored body had been eager to learn and his tenderness had given way to a fierce passion that should have shocked her but had only made her love him more.

Unfortunately their arrival back in London had signalled the end of the fantasy. Luc was always busy and always with Robyn, and Emily had resented the elegant American's close relationship with her husband as she'd struggled to fit in to her new life. As her insecurity grew so did the rows, but six months after the wedding Luc suddenly announced he had a break in his busy work schedule and was taking her on a belated honeymoon. It should have been an ideal time to repair the holes in their marriage, but instead the queasiness she had been suffering from for the past few weeks increased and on arrival at their remote island destination, she fainted. A result of dehydration and hormones, the doctor cheerfully informed her before he dropped the bombshell that she was expecting a baby and one glance at Luc's shocked face warned her that the fairy-tale was over. The moment he discovered she was pregnant their marriage died.

'We'll be landing in an hour,' Luc suddenly informed her, his cold, clipped tone interrupting her thoughts, although he barely bothered to lift his eyes from his computer screen as he addressed her. 'I'm sure you remember the way to the bathroom.'

'I don't need it, thank you,' she replied, stung by his indifference. This time he did look up, his brows raised fractionally in disdain.

'You need to tidy yourself up,' he told her bluntly, unmoved by the stain of colour that flooded her cheeks. 'You'll find your luggage in the bedroom. Hopefully you have something to wear in that vast suitcase that is a little less loud.'

'I'm afraid not,' Emily said sweetly, her chin coming up. 'The larger suitcase contains Jean-Claude's clothes, and this is one of my more discreet outfits.'

'Then we need to go shopping as a matter of urgency. You look like a tramp,' he told her, calmly ignoring her gasp of outrage. 'Your gaudy clothes might be suitable wear for an artists' commune but you are not a hippy—you are my wife and I expect you to dress accordingly.'

'You can go to hell. I'd rather run around naked than allow you to buy my clothes,' Emily snapped furiously, and his mouth curved into an insolent smile that still did strange things to her insides.

'An interesting idea for when we are alone perhaps, but I don't think the villagers of sleepy Montiard are ready for such avant-garde behaviour.'

The temptation to wipe the mockery from his face was so strong that Emily folded her arms across her chest. How dared he say she looked gaudy in a tone that patently meant cheap? Her self-confidence took a nosedive and she quailed beneath his contemptuous gaze. She had been so busy helping Laura at the farmhouse that she had regained her prepregnancy figure without even noticing. She looked good, she reassured herself, and the attention she'd received from a couple of the artists at San Antonia had been a welcome boost, but Luc was usually surrounded by beautiful women who were effortless chic and she felt as gauche as when she had first met him.

Furiously she blinked back the sudden rush of tears, aware that meeting Luc again was nothing like her daydreams. She had often fantasised about bumping into him at some glamorous function and had pictured herself looking stunningly sexy, escorted by her equally gorgeous lover, while Luc looked on and cursed the fact that he had let her go. The dream was stupidly unrealistic, of course, especially the part about the lover. The only man she had ever wanted was as indifferent to her as he had been when she'd left him, and it was ridiculous to feel so hurt.

'I'm not planning on staying at your château for a day

longer than I have to,' she told him icily, 'and I certainly won't
be spending any time alone with you, so you can forget the idea
about me sharing your bed. You can't force me to stay,' she
added, aware that for some reason she wanted to antagonise
him, perhaps because a row would guarantee his attention.

'You think not?' he drawled, patently unmoved by her
anger, and the hint of amusement in his voice caused her
temper to ignite.

'What do you propose to do, lock me in an ivory tower
while you travel the world on endless business commitments?
Maybe you'll come home one day to find that I've gone and
taken Jean-Claude with me,' she taunted.

'I wouldn't try it, *chérie,* because I swear I will hunt you
down and when I find you, you'll wish you'd never crossed me.'

The amusement had gone. Luc was deadly serious, Emily
realised with a shiver at the implicit threat in his voice. He
had made it plain that he was only taking her to France
because Jean-Claude needed her, but it seemed that he
intended to hold her as his prisoner.

Muttering something about needing to freshen up, she
jumped to her feet. She was fully aware of the location of
the opulent bedroom and adjoining bathroom and stumbled
down the aisle, desperate to be alone while she came to
terms with the way her life seemed to be falling apart. Luc
had once spent an entire flight to Mexico making love to
her on the vast double bed, she remembered painfully, but
that had been early on, before the rot had set in and
poisoned their relationship. She hated him, she reminded
herself as she splashed cold water on her face and freed her
hair from the yellow band so that it fell in a swathe of
heavy silk down her back. She didn't know why she had
bothered to speak to him. It was useless when he was in

such an unreasonable mood and she should have remembered that in a verbal sparring match his acidic tongue always left her raw.

What was happening to her? she wondered miserably. Where was the strong, confident woman who had discovered her own sense of self-worth amid the artists at San Antonia? A few hours ago she had been in charge of her life, prepared to seek Luc out and offer him the chance to build a relationship with his son, but now suddenly he had the upper hand and she was out of options.

She emerged from the bathroom to find him stretched out on the bed, his arms folded behind his head as he surveyed her like a sultan might have inspected his latest concubine. It didn't help that he was so gorgeous, she thought helplessly as her eyes were drawn to the muscled hardness of his thighs beneath his superbly cut grey trousers. He had discarded his jacket and his shirt was unbuttoned at the throat to reveal a glimpse of dark hair that she knew covered the whole of his chest. For a moment she closed her eyes, remembering the last time she had seen him stretched out on that bed. Then he had been gloriously and unashamedly naked and she had revelled in the feel of his body on hers, skin on skin, his rough thighs rubbing erotically against the softness of hers.

Too much recall, she thought frantically as her eyes flew open, her cheeks scarlet as she met his sardonic gaze.

'I'd appreciate some privacy,' she told him coolly. 'What do you want?'

'To prove a point perhaps,' he replied, so softly it was as if he was talking to himself, 'or maybe it's just because I can't keep away, which makes me all kinds of a fool,' he added with a harsh laugh.

'You're talking in riddles.' Unwittingly she had edged

closer to the bed, drawn to him with the deadly fascination of a moth to a bright light, and suddenly his hand shot out to capture her wrist.

'Why did you leave me?' The question surprised her but it was not as shocking as when he swung his legs over the side of the bed and pulled her onto his lap.

'You know why,' she muttered, frantically trying to escape. Already she could feel the warmth of his thighs burn through her thin skirt and she shifted uncomfortably as heat coursed through her. This close she could see the fine lines around his eyes, the faint shadow on his jaw, and his mouth was only inches from hers, a wicked temptation she had to fight at all costs.

'I want you to spell it out,' he said, but the grip of his hands on her waist belied the blandness of his tone and she swallowed nervously.

'I'd had enough of being humiliated by you.'

'When did I ever humiliate you?' he growled savagely, and she winced as his fingers bit into her skin. 'You left me without a backward glance. Do you have any idea what my life was like after you disappeared so spectacularly?' he demanded icily. 'One minute we were an apparently happy couple, looking forward to the birth of our first child and then suddenly you were gone, leaving a brief note to say you were leaving me but no further explanation and no indication of when, or indeed if, you intended to come back.

'The Chelsea set had a field day as the weeks passed and it became obvious that I didn't have a clue where you were,' he snapped, and for the first time she began to appreciate the full extent of his anger.

'You could have told people I was visiting my family in Hampshire,' Emily muttered, and received a scathing look.

'Your selfishness is astounding,' he told her bitterly. 'You didn't spare your family a second thought, did you? You didn't think for a moment that they would also be worried about you.'

'My mother knew our marriage was in trouble,' Emily admitted huskily. 'I told her I was going to stay with friends for a while and she wasn't very happy about it. She warned me that millionaires don't grow on trees and said I was a fool. Apparently it's not uncommon for men to play away while their wives are pregnant,' she added, her scathing glance telling him that she did not share Sarah's view. 'But I had concrete proof that you had spent the night with Robyn and I was so sickened by your deceit I knew I couldn't stay with you, carrying on the act that we had a marriage made in heaven, for another minute.'

'I never slept with her. It was all in your imagination,' Luc replied grittily, but she refused to be intimidated by the flash of fire in his eyes.

'You spent the night with her when you came back from Australia. You'd phoned your housekeeper to say you'd delayed your flight for twenty-four hours, but I never received the message and went to the airport to meet you. I saw you, Luc,' she said bitterly, fighting the stab of pain that the memory still evoked. 'You and Robyn. You didn't see me but I'm not stupid. You had your arm around her and it was quite obvious that you'd lied about your change of flights in order to spend one more night with her.'

'And that's the reason you walked out on me? I lost the first year of my son's life because of a mix-up over flights?' The stark incredulity in Luc's voice caused Emily to try and wriggle off his knee but his grip instantly tightened.

'There were reasons why I…lied about the day I was coming home,' he said tightly, patently making a huge effort to control his anger, 'reasons that I would have explained if you'd given me the chance. Instead, you bolted like an immature child. You, *chérie,* took my son. You put me through months of hell and still you wonder that I'm *angry?*' He looked as though he was about to explode, his face a taut mask of barely restrained fury, and Emily shrank from his palpable aggression.

'I know what I saw,' she muttered stubbornly. 'You shared a closeness with Robyn that excluded anyone else, including me.'

'She's my sister-in-law. I've known her for years and I admit I'm fond of her. She went through hell when Yves was killed, not least because she was driving the car and blamed herself for the accident.' He caught hold of her chin so that she was forced to look at him and she was struck by the fierce gleam in his eyes, the determination to make her believe him.

It was the first time they had ever spoken properly about Robyn, the first time either of them had ever really listened. Before, she had allowed her suspicions about his relationship with his PA to fester until they'd boiled over in a torrent of wild accusations that he had refused to dignify with a reply. Instead, he had withdrawn into himself and treated her with such icy disdain that she had shrivelled while her insecurities had multiplied.

'I swear I have never been unfaithful to you, with Robyn or anyone else,' he told her, and the quiet intensity of his voice caused a little bubble of hope to grow in her chest.

Could he really be telling the truth? Had she misread the signs that she had believed pointed to his guilt? She had been so ready to assume the worst, she thought painfully. At the back of her mind she had always thought he would grow tired of her and she had been waiting, looking for proof that he'd regretted marrying her. Had she jumped on the signs of his supposed infidelity as an excuse to leave him before he'd become bored of her, and if that was true, hadn't she denied him the first year of his son's life because of her pride?

It was not a comfortable thought and she shifted on his lap and then wished she hadn't. Their position was way too intimate and it was hard to think straight when her senses were drugged by the musk of his aftershave. Emily needed to put some space between them and the glint in his eyes warned her he was aware of the reason for her escape bid.

'But the night you spent at her flat?' she demanded feverishly, still unwilling to accept she had been wrong all this time. 'I know you were with her.'

'That's right, I spent the entire night trying to sleep on a sofa designed for a midget, counting the hours until I could get home to you. I knew your ultrasound scan was booked for later that day and despite your accusations, I was desperate to go with you.'

'Then why didn't you?' Emily snapped, her tone plainly disbelieving and he sighed.

'As you know, Robyn was once a top model and like many celebrities she's hounded by the press. The day we flew back from Australia she received a tip-off that some risqué photographs she had posed for early in her career were being circulated on the internet, along with accusations that she had been drinking on the night of the accident. She was distraught,' Luc said quietly. 'She begged me to stay with her and we talked for hours about Yves and how much she still missed him. I wanted to come to the hospital with you the next day but I was afraid to leave her while she was talking about ending her life.' He could not have borne another suicide on his conscience, he thought bleakly, but since he'd been forced to make a stark choice between his wife and his sister-in-law he had suffered the punishment of the damned.

'But why did you lie about changing your flight?' Emily faltered, and he met her gaze with eyes that were as cool and clear as a mountain stream.

'Because I knew you'd immediately jump to the wrong conclusion. I wanted desperately to see you after three weeks apart, but Robyn needed me more than she ever had and, God forgive me, I couldn't let her down.'

He had to be telling the truth. No one could lie that convincingly, Emily thought, and her heart flipped with a feeling that was part joy, part despair that she had got it so incredibly wrong. If only she had confronted him instead of running away to lick her wounds. Luc had accused her of behaving like a silly child and she was filled with shame that she had misjudged him so badly. Was it possible that she had been wrong to think he hadn't wanted their baby either? From the minute he'd arrived at San Antonia he had insisted that he wanted to be involved in his son's life, so much so that he was prepared to install her in his château just because Jean-Claude needed her.

For a few glorious seconds hope began to unfurl inside her that there was a chance they could salvage their marriage after all, but then reality bounced back and with it bitter disillusionment. If Luc really felt nothing for his sister-in-law other than affection, why had he installed her in the Chelsea penthouse soon after the break-up of their marriage, and why had he allowed Robyn to send her and Jean-Claude away the day she had tried to see him?

'Nice try, Luc,' Emily flung at him as she tried in vain to slide off his knee. 'For a minute you almost had me convinced.'

'Are you saying you doubt my word?' The note of incredulity in his voice would have been funny if Emily had felt like laughing, but she doubted she would ever smile again. He was so arrogant, she thought furiously, to believe she was still the shy girl he had married.

'Give me one reason why I should believe anything you say?'

'Because you are my wife.'

That couldn't be a flash of hurt in his eyes, she reassured herself. It was impossible to inflict pain on granite and she hardened her heart against him.

'I may have married you but I never gave you the right to tell me how to think. I know for a fact that you're lying, but you can't fool me any more. I'm not the pushover I used to be,' she finished proudly, but his lazy smile caused a flicker of apprehension in the pit of her stomach.

'Really? Perhaps I should put that to the test, *ma chérie*,' he murmured silkily. 'I could never resist a challenge.' Any more than he could resist her, he thought grimly. How dared she accuse him of lying, in that prim, holier-than-thou tone! He had done his best to explain about Robyn but he would be damned if he would try again. Besides, he was tired of talking. They were going round in the same circles as they had a year ago and talking had never got them anywhere then, either. There was only one place where the lines of communication between them were clear and despite her protestations of maidenly outrage he could see the flare of excitement in her eyes. She might refuse to admit, even to herself, that she wanted him, but there was only one reason why she would challenge him and he wouldn't disappoint her.

He moved abruptly and before Emily could guess his intention Luc flipped her back onto the bed, his hard body instantly covering hers so that she was trapped.

'Let me go!' Her anger was tempered with another, more unwelcome emotion as she acknowledged that the feel of his thighs pressing against hers was sending heat coursing through her body. He was so big, so dominantly male, and it had been so long since she had been held in his arms. Already she could feel her resistance fading as sensation took over, but from somewhere she found the strength to push against his shoulders. 'Touch me and I'll scream,' she threatened, and he had the audacity to laugh, his warm breath stirring the tendrils of her hair that curled around her ear. 'Do you want the cabin crew to barge in?' she demanded desperately as he caught hold of her wrists and lifted them above her head so that she was spread helplessly beneath him.

'I would prefer not to have an audience,' he drawled, and she watched, transfixed, as his smile faded, the heat in his eyes a shocking indication of his hunger. He still wanted her! The realisation should have appalled her but instead a soft moan rose in her throat and was captured by his mouth coming down on hers. She was on fire instantly, no thought in her head to deny him when, if she was honest, this was what she had wanted from the moment he had strode towards her at San Antonia.

His tongue pushed insistently against her lips, demanding access, and she parted them with a groan, the thrust of his tongue an erotic invasion that made her twist her hips restlessly against the throbbing proof of his arousal. Where was her pride when she needed it? she thought frantically when he released her mouth at last and proceeded to trail a line of kisses down her neck. Her yellow strap top was a flimsy barrier he quickly dispensed with before pausing for a moment to stare at the vivid orange bra she was wearing underneath.

'An interesting colour combination,' he murmured thickly, and she flushed as sanity seeped back into her brain.

'I like it,' she snapped.

'I like you better without it.' His fingers had already released the clasp and she gasped as he pushed the lacy cups aside to reveal her small, round breasts that were tingling in anticipation of his touch.

They were going to be disappointed, Emily told herself sternly because she refused to give in to the desire that was threatening to engulf her. Much as her body might want him, she could not let Luc make love to her and she glared at him as she tried to drag her arms down from where he had pinioned them above her head.

'I don't know what you're playing at,' she snarled, 'but I don't want to do this.'

'Why, because my touch sickens you?' he queried, his eyes shadowed by his long lashes so that she couldn't read his expression.

'Yes,' she muttered fiercely, but instead of releasing her, his mouth curved into a sardonic smile.

'You're a liar.' He transferred both her wrists into one of his hands and slid the other down to cup her breast, moulding her soft flesh before he stroked his thumb pad across her nipple and watched in apparent fascination as it hardened. 'And you talk too much,' he mocked when at last he lifted his head to stare down into her stunned eyes. 'What happened to my quiet, biddable little wife?'

Biddable! He made her sound like some mindless idiot and she hated the fact that there was a grain of truth in his words. She had loved him so much she would have done anything he'd asked and he had used her weakness for him with ruthless disregard for her feelings.

'I grew up,' she told him icily, 'but I see your chauvinistic attitude towards marriage hasn't improved.'

'*Non,* I demand exclusive possession of my wife,' he said easily. 'You are back where you belong, *chérie,* in my bed, and this time I intend to make sure you stay there.'

Her angry response was cut off by the simple method of his mouth wreaking havoc on hers and by the time he released her she was a quivering mass of emotions. She shivered, unable to control the trembling of her limbs as he cupped her breast in his hand, his olive skin an erotic contrast to the milky whiteness of hers.

His breath was warm and she gasped as she felt the scrape of his jaw against her sensitive flesh. He used his tongue with devastating effect, drawing moist circles around her breast, moving inexorably closer to its centre. She held her breath, every fibre of her being willing him to continue. Finally, when she thought she could bear the waiting no more, his mouth closed fully around the throbbing peak of her nipple and he suckled her.

Instantly sensation coiled in the pit of her stomach and she clung to his shoulders for support as he transferred his mouth to her other breast and administered the same treatment. How had she lived without him? she wondered desperately as the lash of his tongue against her nipple drove her higher and higher. How had she survived for so long without the tumultuous pleasure only he could evoke, and how could she claw back any vestige of her pride when she was fast spinning out of control?

This had to stop, and right now, before she suffered the abject humiliation of begging him to take her. Her body's shameful betrayal was a result of not making love for over a year, she consoled herself when Luc's hand slid beneath her skirt, skimmed her thighs and moved with unerring precision to the core of her femininity. His questing fingers eased the lacy panel of her knickers aside before parting her delicately, the glitter in his eyes as he stared down at her warning her he had discovered the indubitable proof that he turned her on.

Frantically she tried to squeeze her thighs together, determined to deny him access, but her reactions came too late and his fingers slid in deep, a triumphant gleam in his eyes when he found her slick and wet and ready for him. He moved his fingers in an erotic dance and she clenched her teeth, willing her body not to respond, but it felt so wickedly good and already she was aware of the first spasms of pleasure tightening her muscles. Her body was on fire and instinct took over so that she moved her hips restlessly as a wave of intense pleasure engulfed her. Still he continued with his intimate caress, faster, deeper, and she sobbed his name, her cries captured by his mouth as he initiated a kiss that went on and on, his tongue mimicking the movements of his fingers until she lay limply against the pillows, utterly spent.

'So my touch sickens you, does it, *ma petite?*' Luc's dry tone invaded the sensual haze that enveloped her and she winced and closed her eyes against the derision in his. 'You have a peculiar way of showing it.' He swung his legs over the side of the bed and stood looking down at her, a humourless laugh escaping him when she crossed her arms over her brèasts. Her skirt was caught up around her waist and she knew she must look totally disheveled, but he did not appear to have a hair out of place and bore no physical signs of the wild passion they had shared moments before.

It's good to know you've dropped your objections to taking up your role as my wife once more, but we'll be landing in five minutes. I suggest you tidy yourself up before I introduce you to my staff. You look a little…flustered, *ma petite.*'

It was impossible to hate a man more than she loathed and detested Luc Vaillon, Emily decided furiously as she scrambled back into her clothes. She would rather move in with the devil than live with him in his château, she decided as she marched back to her seat, her head held high, and the fact that the members of Luc's staff studiously avoided her gaze only added to her humiliation. She felt like a cheap tart and she was determined not to put herself in that position again, but even as she made the resolution her heart skittered in her chest.

Jean-Claude was awake, sitting on his father's knee and staring up at him with wide-eyed fascination, and for the first time she truly appreciated the extent of Luc's power over her. For some reason he had decided he wanted to be a father to their son after all and she did not underestimate his ruthless determination to get his own way. He had told her she could live at the château for as long as Jean-Claude depended on her, but that would be years. At what age did a child no longer need its mother? she wondered. Nothing would ever induce her to leave her son but the cost to her self-respect could be immense, especially if Luc demanded that she resume her role as his wife for the duration of her stay.

He couldn't force her, she reassured herself, but she'd just proved that he didn't have to. She was her own worst enemy where her husband was concerned, and from now on she would have to be on her guard.

CHAPTER FOUR

THE LOIRE REGION of France was lush and green, in stark contrast to the rocky, arid landscape that Emily had grown accustomed to at San Antonia. The car followed the route of the river before the road began to climb steeply and she drew a sharp breath as imposing grey stone walls rose up in front of them.

'You want Jean-Claude to grow up *here?*' she queried faintly as they drove through an arched gateway cut into the outer defensive wall and into a wide courtyard. 'It looks…medieval!'

'It is. The Château Montiard was built in the fifteenth century although only the outer wall and towers and the wine cellars remain of the original building. And the dungeon,' Luc added and she threw him a startled glance, searching for signs of humour and finding none. 'The main residence has been expertly modernised and I designed Jean-Claude's nursery myself. He will want for nothing,' he said pointedly, and Emily wondered if he was hinting that she would be expected to sleep in the scullery. 'The château has been in the Vaillon family's possession since it was acquired by them in 1506. It is Jean-Claude's birthright, his heritage—something you should understand when your own family has such strong links with Heston Grange.'

'How did the Vaillons acquire the château?' she asked curiously, and Luc shrugged.

'By force, I imagine. My forefathers were brigands, although history has it that René Vaillon had some kind of hold over the original owner and blackmailed him into allowing René to marry his daughter. The story goes that the girl was distraught at being forced to wed the boorish René and refused to sleep with him. To punish her, he locked her in the highest tower but, rather than give herself to him, she threw herself from the top. Lucky for you that you have no such inhibitions where sex is concerned, *chérie*.'

'Poor girl,' Emily murmured coolly, ignoring his jibe. 'No woman wants to be married to a barbarian that she has no respect for.'

Luc's jaw tightened ominously and she waited for his temper to erupt, but instead his mouth curved into a grudging smile. *'Touché, ma petite.* You have developed a clever tongue, but perhaps I should remind you that your position here is extremely tenuous. It wouldn't do to upset me.'

'Heaven forbid, I'm aware that you expect your wife to be obedient and *biddable.*'

'Then we should get along just fine.'

He just had to have the last word, Emily thought viciously as she watched him stride across the courtyard to greet a multitude of uniformed staff assembled on the steps leading to the huge central doorway. His secretaries and the nanny had followed from the airport in a second car, and as she freed Jean-Claude from his child seat Liz Crawford appeared, her arms outstretched to take her charge.

'Monsieur Vaillon asked me to take the baby straight up to

the nursery while he introduces you to his household,' she explained apologetically and Emily's heart sank. During their brief conversation on the flight from Spain she had warmed to Liz, who had explained that she had returned to child care after her husband had died and her daughters were both busy with their own lives. 'I appreciate that no one can take your place as Jean-Claude's mother, and of course you want to do everything for him,' she had murmured sympathetically, 'but your husband explained that you've been ill and babies can be exhausting. I'm here to give you a break when you need it.'

On the surface it sounded reasonable, but Emily had her doubts. Liz was kind and motherly but ultimately she was answerable to Luc and she would follow his orders, even if that meant unwittingly engineering a separation between Jean-Claude and his mother.

She was quaking inside as she crossed the courtyard to where Luc and his staff were waiting and wished she had followed his order to change into something slightly less colourful. As her bright orange skirt danced in the breeze she felt like a peacock at a funeral and Luc's jaw tightened ominously when she joined him on the steps. If possible, she was even lovelier than when he had first met her, he thought, noting the way the sunlight made her skirt appear almost transparent so that the outline of her slender figure was displayed.

He wasn't the only one to notice, either, he realised as he subjected a young groom to a fulminating glare. Perhaps his ancestor René had had the right idea by locking his young bride in the tower, away from other admirers, but the thought did not improve his temper and he stiffened as a sudden gust of wind blew Emily's hair across his face. It smelt of lemons, fresh and enticing, and he fought the urge to wrap the strands around his fingers, tilt her head and take possession of her mouth in a way that would leave the cocky groom in no doubt that she was Madame Vaillon, his wife.

Emily pushed her hair over her shoulders, aware that the members of Luc's household staff were staring at her curiously. No doubt they had expected his wife to be elegant and sophisticated, but beset by nerves she could only drum up a shy smile when he introduced his butler, Philippe, who together with his wife, Sylvie, and their daughter, Simone, organised the running of the château.

'You could at least try to act a little more friendly,' Luc muttered as she followed him into the vast, marble-floored entrance hall. 'Philippe's family have worked at the château for generations. Their history goes back almost as far as the Vaillons' and I expect you to treat them with the courtesy they deserve, not to act like a haughty English princess.'

'I wasn't being haughty,' Emily defended herself, 'but I'm not used to living with dozens of staff. Heston Grange cost so much to run that my parents could only afford to employ our lovely old housekeeper, Betty. I don't know how you expect me to act, or even what my roll at the château is. You introduced me as your wife, but I still can't believe you expect me to resume our relationship as if nothing has happened.'

'Believe, *ma petite,*' Luc suggested grimly, his expression unfathomable, and she sighed and glanced around the wide hallway.

Although the château seemed imposing from the outside, inside it was light and airy, with sunlight streaming in through the tall windows to bounce off the mellow oak panelling and creamy-coloured walls. Far from being cold and austere, much care had been taken to make it a comfortable family residence and she warmed to its charm, feeling instantly at

home, which was curious when she had always felt uncomfortable at Heston. There was no point in growing attached
to the château, she reminded herself, she wouldn't be staying
long.

Her eyes turned to the many portraits that adorned the
walls, some of which were obviously very old and no doubt
priceless.

'Meet the family,' Luc quipped as he followed her gaze.
'There are paintings of every one of my ancestors, the most
recent being this one of my parents.'

Jean-Louis Vaillon and his wife, Céline, stared down at
Emily disdainfully and she shivered. Was it simply the style
of the painting, or were they really as cold and unfriendly as
they looked? Luc bore a strong resemblance to his handsome
father but Jean-Louis's eyes were flat and devoid of any
emotion while Luc's burned with fire—usually brought on by
anger at her, Emily conceded sadly, although there had been
times in the past when he had looked at her with an expression that she could almost believe was tenderness.

'Do your parents live here at the château?' she asked ap-
prehensively, but he shook his head.

'They're both dead. As you might have guessed from the
painting, it wasn't a happy marriage, more of a business arrangement between two wealthy families. My mother's
family owned the vineyards that are now part of the Vaillon
estate.'

'But they didn't love each other?' Emily murmured, and
Luc gave a harsh laugh.

'Definitely not. My father was a cold, remote man and my
mother was sensitive and for the most part deeply unhappy.
She was fascinated by the story about old René and his tragic
wife, so much so that she felt compelled to re-enact history.'

His words took a few seconds to sink in and Emily frowned. 'You mean your mother jumped to her death from one of the towers?' she queried, unable to disguise the shock in her voice. 'How terrible! How old were you?'

'Fifteen or so,' he replied with a shrug. 'I don't remember exactly.'

But the bleakness in his eyes told a different story and Emily guessed that every detail of the tragic event was etched on his brain.

'That's awful,' she whispered. 'I can't believe a mother would leave her child.' At fifteen Luc would still have needed the love and protection of his parents. Her heart ached for him, knowing in his eyes she'd kept his son away from him, too. Was the tragedy of his past a reason for his reluctance to show his emotions? she wondered, her heart aching for him. 'It must have been grim for whoever discovered her,' she added, and Luc stared at her, a nerve jumping in his cheek.

'Yes, it wasn't a pretty sight.'

'You mean you… Oh, Luc!' It didn't matter that they were sworn enemies. All Emily could picture was Luc as a teenager, a boy on the brink of adulthood with his emotions all over the place. His mother's horrific suicide must have marked him for life, yet from the look of his stern father he would have received little sympathy or understanding for his terrible loss. 'Why did you never say anything?' she murmured, reaching her hand out to him in an involuntary gesture, wanting to comfort him. 'In all the months that we were married, you never mentioned your parents.' And she had been too shy, too unsure of him, to pry into his private life.

Luc glanced down at her hand on his arm, his expression so coolly aloof that she withdrew, her face burning. His body language could not have shouted more loudly that she was invading his personal space. He neither expected nor wanted her sympathy and her blood chilled. She had been an outsider when he'd married her and nothing had changed. She would do well to remember that fact.

'Revealing the curse of the Vaillon wives hardly seemed appropriate on our wedding day, *chérie*. Marriages in my family seem to have the unhappy knack of ending in tragedy. For Jean-Claude's sake, let's hope ours doesn't suffer the same fate.'

'It already has,' Emily pointed out. 'Cupid's arrow was way off target when he brought us together, and now it's damaged beyond repair.' She gave a sigh of frustration when Luc made no reply and simply stared at her as if intent on reading her mind. 'This isn't going to work, Luc. There's too much bitterness and mistrust between us to try and kick-start our marriage. Perhaps I should start looking for a house in the village for Jean-Claude and me. Somewhere close enough for you to visit him easily.'

'Forget it,' Luc told her bluntly, and she watched impotently as he strode towards the wide staircase. 'You can look for a property in the village by all means, but my son stays here, and he certainly won't be alone. I intend to make the château my permanent base, both to live and work. Believe me, from now on Jean-Claude will have my undivided attention.'

'But what about your travels, your endless commitments and meetings in every corner of the globe?' Emily queried, a note of panic entering her voice. 'You can hardly take him into the boardroom with you.'

'I'm cutting right back on my travels. I admit I'm not finding the art of delegation easy but it's a small sacrifice when I have my son.'

'A sacrifice you refused to make for me,' Emily accused bitterly. 'Have you any idea how lonely I felt during our marriage? You dumped me in the middle of a big city where I had no friends and the only time I ever saw you was in bed. We never talked, Luc,' she said miserably. 'We never did all the normal things most couples do, like…I don't know, go to the supermarket together.'

'I employed an excellent housekeeper to take care of the running of the penthouse so that you didn't have to,' he snapped. 'And what's romantic about shopping for groceries?'

'At least it would have been better than those agonising dinner parties Robyn arranged. The few times we could have spent the evening together were hijacked by entertaining your business associates.'

'I thought you would appreciate the chance to socialise,' he muttered. 'You had unlimited access to my credit cards to go shopping for new outfits—and most women like to dress up,' he added in a tone that patently spoke of his frustration that he did not understand her.

And therein was the root of many of their problems, Emily thought sadly. She was nothing like Luc's previous lovers. It was a mystery why he had ever married her and his determination to keep her his wife was even more puzzling.

'You can't force me to stay here,' she warned and he shrugged, as if he was bored with the whole subject.

'No, but I can ensure that you never set a foot outside the château with my son,' he said coldly, and the implicit threat in his voice caused a shiver to run the length of her spine. He knew she wouldn't leave her baby. It was emotional blackmail of the worst kind and she was trapped.

Luc continued with his journey up the stairs, rounded a

corner and disappeared from view, but Emily stumbled after him, halting before a huge canvas that took centre stage at the top of the first main flight of stairs. The portrait was of a woman, the style of painting and her clothing suggesting that the picture was a recent addition to the Vaillon archives, but something about her face captured Emily's attention. She, whoever she was, was the most beautiful woman Emily had ever seen, with classically sculptured bone structure and lux-uriant black hair that gleamed like raw silk.

Was she one of the cursed Vaillon wives or a relative from Luc's own side of the family? Certainly she had the air of dis-dainful hauteur that hinted at her French aristocracy, her dark eyes as cold and lacking in emotion as the painting of Luc's parents. To Emily, the woman summed up everything she was not. She was elegant and exquisite and she looked as though she belonged in the château, which only emphasised the point that she herself, in her cheap, colourful clothes, was a rank outsider. She had no place here, and living in a remote French château would in many ways be even worse than when they had lived in the Chelsea penthouse. She would have no chance to make friends or have a life of her own. She would be totally dependent on Luc and the idea terrified her.

She hurried up the stairs that Luc had taken minutes before and arrived on a long landing where a window at one end allowed sunlight to stream in. It was like a scene from *Alice in Wonderland,* she thought hysterically as she ran the length of the landing, finding that the doors on either side of her were firmly shut. The last one had been left slightly ajar and she pushed it open, her breath catching in her throat as she glanced around the vast room.

With its dark wood floor, panelling and ceiling, the room could have appeared gloomy, but the whole of one wall held the same enormous windows that she had noted on the landing. On the opposite wall was a magnificent fireplace and above it a stunning tapestry that she guessed was a priceless antique from the château's past. It was not the décor or the artwork that made Emily stare, however, but the sight of the huge, ornately carved four-poster bed that stood on a raised platform in the centre of the room. Instinct told her the bed was an intrinsic part of the château and her eyes were drawn to the coat of arms that had again been worked in tapestry and which hung around the top of the bed above the rich velvet drapes.

Had the despicable René insisted that his terrified bride join him on this bed? Emily wondered with a shiver. Had Luc's unhappy mother slept in this room, until she had been drawn to end her life rather than remain at the château any longer?

'Luc!' Ghosts from the past seemed to lurk in every corner of the room and with a cry Emily spun round, catching the sounds of a modern power shower that was a welcome intrusion on her imagination. 'We have to talk.'

The bathroom adjoining the master bedroom was a clever compromise between the château's historical past and modern requirements, and although the enormous bath set on its carved, gold-plated feet dominated the room, the shower cubicle at one end did not seem out of place.

'Are you listening?' she demanded of the shadowy figure whose outline was just visible through the frosted glass. 'As you're so keen to point out, I am your wife and as such I have rights, too. The days when women were treated no better than cattle and were viewed as their husband's possession are over. I'm not the feeble, frightened girl that René's wife must have been and I won't allow you to bully me!'

'Bully you!' There was a volcanic eruption from the shower and Emily took a hasty step backward, away from the door, but she was too late. The glass doors separated and one wet, hair-roughened arm snaked out to drag her into the cubicle where the powerful spray soaked her clothes in seconds. 'My restraint where you're concerned has been nothing short of saintly,' Luc informed her furiously, as Emily backed up against the tiled wall.

Saintly was not a word she would have used to describe him, she thought faintly as her eyes were drawn to his magnificent, naked body, watching the way the soap suds clustered amid the hairs that covered his chest and trailed down over his hips to the powerful muscles of his thighs. He was sinfully gorgeous with a body that would incite the most ardent saint to think wicked thoughts. Hers must have been transparently visible in her wide, shocked eyes as she continued to stare at him, transfixed by the hardness of his shaft that lifted and swelled to burgeoning, throbbing arousal.

'*Mon Dieu,* I don't need this,' he muttered, and her startled gaze swung to his face to see a tide of colour stain his cheekbones. 'Stop looking at me like that, *ma chérie,* unless you are prepared to take the consequences.'

'I'm not looking at you like anything,' she snapped, desperate to disguise her excitement as heat coursed through her. 'You pulled me in here. I can't help it if your body is…'

'Hot? Hard? There's no dispute on that one, is there?' he taunted as he stood barricading the door of the shower, his legs apart, gloriously unashamed of the potent force of his arousal. 'Desperate to finish what we started on the plane? Is that why you're here, Emily? Foreplay wasn't enough and it left you aching for my full possession? You don't have to worry,' he assured her silkily as he moved towards her with deliberate intent. 'I'm more than willing to help you over-come your reluctance to resume your role as my wife.' He gave a harsh laugh, his derision directed solely at himself. You always did unman me, *chérie*. I have never needed any woman the way I need you.'

'Luc, no!' with the tiny part of her brain that was still functioning, Emily fought against the overpowering chemical reaction between them, which was adding to the steamy atmosphere of the shower cubicle. As he pulled her up against his chest he turned off the tap and she gasped, shamefully aware that her nipples were prominently displayed beneath her clingy wet top and her skirt was moulded to her thighs. 'I came in here to talk about Jean-Claude,' she muttered, her eyes focused on his mouth as he lowered his head towards her. 'I don't want this.'

'*Chérie,* you're gagging for it,' he said bluntly, and she shuddered at the crudity of his words. Where was her pride? she demanded frantically, but then his mouth captured hers in a kiss that stole her sanity and drove every other thought but her driving need for him out of her mind. He removed her wet clothes with deft movements, his lips never leaving hers and she trembled at that first touch of his naked skin against hers, the hard sinew of his thighs pressing on the softness of hers as he pushed her up against the shower wall.

She should stop him. Every instinct warned her that she was following a path she would later regret but the burning fire in his eyes set her alight. Gone was the cold, aloof busi-nessman she had felt so in awe of, in his place the passion-ate Frenchman who in the first weeks and months of their marriage had been unable to keep his hands off her. She revelled in the fact that his control was teetering on the brink. It made her feel feminine, desirable, all the things she hadn't felt since she had fallen pregnant with Jean-Claude and Luc had retreated from her, both physically and emotionally.

'You want this every bit as much as I do,' he breathed as he trailed his lips to her ear where he nipped the sensitive lobe with his sharp teeth before sliding lower to her throat and finally her breasts, taking one throbbing nipple and then the other into his mouth.

Emily wanted to deny his taunt but she was helpless, sucked into a vortex of exquisite sensation so that she dug her fingers into his hair to hold him to his task. She trembled when he moved lower still, the muscles in her stomach quivering as his tongue dipped into her naval, created havoc, and then continued on his relentless path to the junction between her thighs. He wouldn't, she thought dizzily as her legs buckled and he supported her weight while his lips moved over her wet curls until his tongue was able to explore her in an intimate caress that heightened her arousal to fever pitch.

Suddenly he straightened and, before she had time to guess his intentions, lifted her into his arms so that she was forced to curl her legs around his thighs, feeling the solid strength of his erection push against her belly. With his hands cupping her bottom, he stepped out of the cubicle and strode into the bedroom, halting by the huge bed. Emily opened her eyes as reality intruded with a vengeance.

'This is where I should have brought you on our wedding night, where all the Vaillon wives have given themselves totally and utterly to their husbands,' Luc told her, his eyes glittering, and she recognised that he was fast approaching the point of no return. 'If I take you now, on this bed, I can never let you go; you will for ever be mine. You have about thirty seconds to stop me, *ma petite*,' he warned her, but Emily was lost. This was Luc, the man she had once loved, still loved if she had the courage to look into her heart. His hard arousal was pulsating against her thighs and with no other thought than that she needed him, she wriggled lower down his body, her legs still wrapped tightly around him.

Luc muttered an imprecation in his own tongue as he lowered her onto the edge of the bed, his hands beneath her bottom lifting her as he entered her with one powerful thrust that made her gasp. It had been a long time and she closed her eyes as he filled her, waited a second for her muscles to relax around him before he withdrew, only to thrust again, deeper this time, the sensations he aroused in her unbearably intense. It was no gentle seduction. Gone was Luc the skilful, controlled lover, in his place a man intent on assuaging a driving need that had been building for over a year. He took her with a hunger, a savagery that made her tremble, although not with fear, but an answering passion that she was powerless to deny.

She clung to his shoulders as lowered his head once more to take her mouth in a fierce kiss that warned of his ultimate possession, and all the time his body moved within hers, hard against soft, dark olive skin an erotic contrast to the milky whiteness of her thighs. On, on, higher and higher he drove her and she could only hang on for dear life as waves of sensation built inexorably, reached their peak and sent her crashing over the edge, her body shuddering as she drowned in pleasure.

He was mere seconds behind her, his brow beaded with sweat, and she stared at him poised above her, his face a rigid mask as he fought to stem the tide of pleasure that threatened to engulf him. 'Emily...' Her name was wrenched from his throat and once again she marvelled at his total loss of control where once his restraint had been so absolute. His aim may have been to humiliate her but there were no winners in this power struggle, only losers, she thought, blinking back the sudden rush of tears.

Their bodies might be satiated, still trembling with the last aftershocks of their mutual climax, but it had been sex at its most primitive, the need to appease a basic urge. At least for him it was, she conceded sadly. He did not confuse lust with love but for her they were inextricably linked and although her body was replete her heart ached and over-spilled with the words he didn't want to hear.

'I think that proves we can dispense with the idea of divorce once and for all, don't you?' The hint of smug satisfaction in Luc's voice demolished the remnants of her self-respect, and she wrapped her arms around her body in a purely defensive gesture. 'I have to admit I found your dedication to duty impressive.'

'I don't give a damn what you think,' Emily told him tightly, her voice thick with tears she was desperate to hide from him. For a moment he stilled and she felt his eyes on her, although she refused to turn her head and look at him.

'Emily…' There was a curious huskiness in his voice but she steeled herself to ignore it. Luc had been hewn from the same stone as his medieval château and any hint of softness was in her imagination only.

'Go to hell,' she told him succinctly. 'You've got what you wanted and so have I. Let's just leave it at that shall we? Quits.'

For one terrifying moment she thought he would join her on the bed and she silently prayed that he would leave her before she broke down. Her tears would be the final humiliation. She couldn't bear him to see her cry and she released her breath on a slow hiss when he eventually moved away.

'As you wish, *chérie*. I suggest you remain here and rest. You look…shattered,' he commented silkily as he strode towards the *en suite,* 'and Robyn has organised a small reception for tonight, a chance for you to meet some of my friends who live locally. Everyone is curious to see the new mistress of the Château Montiard,' he added as Emily stared at him, unable to conceal her dismay.

'You mean Robyn's *here?*'

'Naturellement,' he replied with a shrug that screamed of his indifference to her reaction. 'Where else would she be?'

'Where else indeed?' Emily muttered thickly, shocked not so much by his announcement but by this open display of his cruelty and the level of her pain. Robyn, one of the most stunningly beautiful women of her generation and indubitably Luc's lover, was here at the château and any tenuous hopes she might have harboured about her relationship with her husband drained away.

Luc halted in the doorway to the bathroom and gave an impatient sigh. 'I've explained that my work base is now here at the château and Robyn is my personal assistant. I rely heavily on her organisational skills so try not to let your vivid imagination run away with you, *ma petite.*'

Emily's brows shot skywards and she called on every ounce of her acting ability as she surveyed Luc with cool disdain. 'I'm sure her organisational skills are the least of her charms, but have it your own way. One thing, though, which of us will you introduce as your *mistress* of the château? I suggest you think about it before you cause your friends embarrassment,' she murmured, and winced as he slammed the door with such force that it shook on its hinges. Only then did she bury her head in the pillows and cry until there were no more tears left. At some point exhaustion took over and she slept, unaware that Luc had returned and stood staring down at her tear-streaked face before he covered her with the quilt and finally left her in peace.

CHAPTER FIVE

THIS DAY SHOULD be forever etched on my mind as the day I had first held my son, Luc brooded. Instead, there was only one person who dominated his thoughts.

Emily.

Her name swirled around in his head, teasing him, tormenting him as she had always done. With a muttered oath he strode into the dining room, recalling with stark clarity the way she had writhed beneath him a few hours earlier. Her hoarse cries as he'd driven her to the pinnacle of sexual pleasure and the way she had sobbed his name with the power of her release were not things he would forget in a hurry and even now, with less than an hour to go before the damned dinner party Robyn had arranged, his body was responding to those memories with an enthusiasm that made him ache. How the hell was he going to sit through dinner like this, when all he really wanted to do was go upstairs and make love to his wife with a thoroughness that would atone for the months they'd spent apart?

Not that he would be welcome, he admitted grimly. He had been every inch the barbarian Emily had accused him of, so driven by his own damnable need that he had been rough with her, maybe had even hurt her. It was not a comfortable thought and he walked over to the window to stare out at the spectacular view across the Loire Valley. Hurting her had not been part of his plan but if he was honest, he didn't have a plan other to reclaim what was rightfully his. It was a frightening admission for a man who exerted supreme control over every aspect of his life. He couldn't remember a time when he had acted on instinct rather than following a preordained programme. He didn't like surprises, which was why he had found his reaction to Lord Anthony Dyer's youngest daughter so startling.

Heston Grange represented one of the finest pieces of real estate in England. It would be a lie to deny that his original interest had been solely in acquiring the magnificent country houses with a view to refurbishment. It would represent a huge coup for his development company, he'd acknowledged, but he had felt some sympathy for the Dyers, who had owned the house for generations.

From the start he had been aware of undercurrents within the family, especially from Anthony's pushy wife Sarah, and he had been mildly amused by the hinted suggestion that marriage to one of the Dyers' daughters could result in a drop in the asking price of the estate. Sarah had been desperate to keep a foothold in the door of Heston Grange and her three older daughters were certainly attractive, but as far as he had been concerned, marriage was not on his agenda.

And then he had met Emily.

Even now, two years on, he could not repress a smile as he recalled his first sight of her. With her flushed cheeks and tangled hair she had reminded him of a wood nymph, her beauty completely natural, earthy and unbelievably sexy. The fact that she had been as shy and awkward as a young colt had only added to his fascination. He'd spent that first evening unable to take his eyes off her and although he had accepted Anthony Dyer's invitation to stay at Heston and discuss the most important business deal of his life, he had found himself drawn with annoying regularity to the stables.

He had needed every ounce of his patience as he'd sought to break down Emily's reserve, he remembered, but she had been worth the wait. The first time he'd kissed her he had shocked them both with the level of his hunger, but far from frightening her she had revealed a hidden depth of passion that had left him mad with longing. There had been no plan in his head, no carefully thought-out decision to ask her to marry him. He had reacted on pure instinct, as if his soul had recognised its mate and could not bear to let her go. But presumably she had not felt the same way, which was why she had left him.

'Will there be anything else, Monsieur Vaillon?' Simone's voice interrupted his thoughts and he swung round, dredging up a smile for the maid. She had finished putting the final touches to the table, checking the cutlery and adjusting the position of the centre display of old-fashioned roses. Their exquisite perfume hung heavy in the air, their petals reflected in the highly polished veneer of the table, and he felt his tension ease a little.

'Everything looks perfect,' he complimented in his own language and Simone blushed with pleasure. He had every confidence that the dinner party would run without a hitch, aided by Sylvie's excellent cooking and Philippe's imperturbable presence at the table, but his main thanks would have to go to his personal assistant.

If only Robyn had consulted him first, before arranging a social event for Emily's first night at the château, he thought grimly. He hadn't expected her to even be here and had assumed she would remain at her Paris apartment where he'd phoned to say he was bringing both Jean-Claude and Emily back to the château.

Why had Robyn immediately driven down? The paperwork she had said was vital had been an excuse, he was sure of it. She had dealt with far more complex affairs without his help before. She better than anyone was aware of the tensions that had existed within his marriage. It was Robyn he had confided in when he had been unable to reveal his innermost fears to Emily. Surely she could appreciate his desire for some time alone with his wife and son?

Perhaps her presence would be a good thing, he mused, a way for him to demonstrate to Emily that there really was nothing going on between him and his PA. But he was tied to Robyn by the past. It had taken her a long time to come to terms with his brother's death, and she relied on him as her emotional prop. It was churlish of him to feel restless but suddenly he wished she would pick up the threads of her life once more and allow him the freedom to carry on with his.

As Simone made to go he called her back. 'I want you to take this up to Madame Vaillon,' he requested, handing the maid a flat box engraved with the name of an exclusive boutique from the nearby city of Orléans. 'It's a present, something for my wife to wear tonight,' he explained. 'My secretary has just returned with it.' Simone nodded, her eyes shining with an excitement he only hoped would be reflected in Emily's blue gaze.

'Madame, it is time for you to wake, I think.'

Emily opened her eyes and stared into the anxious face of Luc's maid.

'It is almost the dinner,' Simone explained agitatedly in her broken English, and slowly Emily sat up. She was in the master bedroom, Luc's bedroom, lying on the vast bed. And she was naked, although fortunately someone had covered her with the heavy silk quilted bedspread. The knowledge did not alleviate her embarrassment and she shuddered as her memory returned. Had Simone discovered her wet clothes in the shower where Luc had stripped her? Had he sent Simone to check on her, perhaps to make sure she hadn't been tempted to throw herself out of the window like two other Vaillon wives before her had done? Heaven knew what the young maid was thinking. Emily groaned as she wrapped the bedspread round her and inched towards the edge of the bed.

'I'll quickly shower and dress,' she explained with a mixture of gestures and her schoolgirl French, and Simone's face cleared.

'Monsieur Vaillon asked me to give you this. His assistant bought it for you,' she said cheerfully, her eyes widening as Emily opened the box to reveal a simple but exquisite sheath of navy blue silk, with delicate shoestring straps and a low-cut bodice.

'*C'est très belle,*' Simone breathed reverently and Emily reluctantly had to agree that Robyn had exemplary taste.

'It's very pretty,' she agreed briskly, replacing the dress between the layers of tissue in the box, 'but I have my own clothes.'

She frowned when she discovered her empty suitcase on a chair and further investigation revealed that her clothes had been hung in one of the wardrobes, her few brightly coloured outfits looking lost and out of place against the backdrop of the grand antique furniture. 'I think I'll wear this,' she said defiantly, selecting her one dress that came anywhere near formal. It was a cerise pink halter neck with a long skirt that looked demure until she moved and revealed a split that reached mid-thigh. Elegant it was not, she conceded, noting Simone's dismayed expression, but it was bright and funky and, more importantly, hers. She refused to wear a dress that had been chosen by Luc's mistress.

'But Monsieur Vaillon—'

'Does not tell me what to wear,' she finished for Simone. 'Did he ask you to hang my clothes in here?' she demanded, and the maid nodded, her confusion palpable when Emily instructed her to transfer all the items in the wardrobe to the empty room across the landing.

'Monsieur Vaillon will not be happy,' Simone muttered, and on that one Emily was forced to agree, but Luc's anger would be vented on her—she could bet on it—not the hapless Simone.

She showered and changed in record time, piling her long chestnut hair into a loose chignon and adding a touch of make-up, emphasising her long eyelashes with mascara and defining her lips with a clear gloss. In the nursery Jean-Claude greeted her enthusiastically and she lifted him into her arms with a sigh of pleasure, rubbing her cheek against his satiny curls.

'I've just given him some yoghurt,' Liz warned. 'He might be a bit sticky and you're all dressed for dinner.'

'I don't care,' Emily returned cheerfully. She would never be one of those mothers who cared more about her appearance than cuddling her baby. 'It's rather late for his teatime,' she commented, and Liz nodded.

'I'm afraid he slept all afternoon and now he's raring to go but I'll play with him while you're busy with your guests.'

'Even better, I'll take him down to meet them,' Emily said

decisively. 'Can you give him the quickest bath on record, while I choose his outfit?'

If Liz was surprised she said nothing, and Emily smiled at her son, her heart clenching with love as she received a cheeky grin in return. She refused to look too closely at her reasons for wanting to take him down to the dinner party. Perhaps it was to emphasise her role in his life to Luc, or maybe it was just because she wanted to show the baby off.

'You are the most gorgeous little man in the whole world,' she told her son a short while later, when Jean-Claude had been bathed and dressed in a smart sailor suit.

'Thank you, *chérie,* but not so little, as I hope I demonstrated earlier,' came a throaty voice in her ear, and her cheeks flamed as she swung round to find Luc close behind her. For a moment she stiffened and then her lips twitched. He was an arrogant devil and she had forgotten how he'd loved to tease her mercilessly, until their shared laughter had slowly died and the chemistry between them had fizzed out of control. Her eyes darkened with an array of emotions she could not disguise and the answering gleam in his grey gaze told her he was aware of her wayward thoughts.

He didn't play fair, she told herself crossly as she swung her back on him and fought to bring her hormones under control.

Resplendent in his black dinner suit and white silk shirt, he looked good enough to eat and she was hungry. Making love with him earlier had whetted her appetite after more than a year apart but it couldn't happen again, she told herself firmly. Luc had to understand that she was an independent woman, not a puppet who would jump when he pulled the strings.

'We must share the same thoughts,' he murmured, and her

cheeks turned scarlet at the very idea of him being party to her fevered imagination. 'I also came to collect Jean-Claude,' he added coolly, lifting the unresisting baby into his arms, and Emily sighed at the look of delight on Jean-Claude's face as he laid his head on Luc's shoulder.

'You're honoured,' she muttered bleakly. 'He doesn't usually take to strangers.'

'But I'm not a stranger, I'm his father,' Luc pointed out quietly. 'Perhaps he recognised me from here, in his heart, in the same way that I recognised with absolute certainty that he is my son.'

Emily was startled by the raw emotion in his voice. The flash of pain in his eyes as he looked down at Jean-Claude was real. No one could act that convincingly. Once again she was filled with guilt that she must have misjudged him. But if that was true, why had he dismissed the chance to see Jean-Claude after his birth? Nothing made sense and she sighed, unaware that he had noted the misery in her eyes.

'Is something troubling you?' he queried politely, as if he were addressing a member of his staff rather than the woman he had made love to so passionately only hours before.

She laughed bitterly. 'Other than being kidnapped and held in your damn great castle against my will, you mean?' she flung at him sarcastically, and his jaw tightened.

'If you insist on leaving, I'll have Philippe drive you to wherever you want to go.'

'But not with Jean-Claude?'

'*Non.*' His reply was cold, unemotional but utterly implacable, and she gave a frustrated sigh.

'You know I'd never leave him.'

'Then it is a prison of your own making, because I will never let you take him again, and if you try…' He broke off and glanced down at the child in his arms, his eyes flaring with a level of emotion he had never awarded her. 'You will be sorry,' he promised flatly, and she shivered at the inherent threat. How had they come to this? she thought miserably as tears stung her eyes.

'Do you ever wish we could turn back the clock?' she whispered, and his harsh laugh scraped across her already raw nerves.

'Every day of my life, *chérie*—and for so many reasons,' he added obliquely, but she was sure he was referring to their marriage, certain he regretted the day he had made her his wife, and all her old insecurities flooded back. 'But unfortunately we cannot change the past. I have missed so much of Jean-Claude's babyhood. Precious time that cannot be replaced, and for what?' He rounded on her bitterly. '*Mon Dieu*, Emily, I am trying very hard to understand where I went wrong, but did my crimes really deserve such a cruel punishment? Do you know what haunts me the most?' he demanded. 'If you hadn't filed for a divorce, I still wouldn't know the whereabouts of my son. Perhaps I should count myself lucky that you only sentenced me to a year of despair. You could have kept him from me for ever.'

'I told you I was coming back to England,' Emily defended herself. 'I wanted us to share custody of Jean-Claude.'

'Only because you were running out of money,' he said scathingly and her head jerked back as if he had struck her.

'That's not true. I don't need money. I don't need anything from you. All I ever wanted was a little of your time,' she muttered thickly. 'I wanted us to build a relationship outside the bedroom but you made me feel as though my only function was to provide convenient sex.'

'Which you hated, I suppose?' he mocked angrily, his eyes flashing fire. She sighed, aware that she wasn't getting through to him. 'I didn't hate it but I was unhappy that it was the only form of communication between us. A marriage can't survive solely on sex, as we discovered once I fell pregnant and you refused to come near me. There was precious little communication between us then, was there Luc?'

'You sound like a spoilt child whingeing for attention,' he ground out furiously as he fought the sharp needles of his conscience that reminded him he hadn't spent enough time with her. He wasn't used to sharing, he acknowledged grimly. He'd got into the habit of compartmentalising his life and when he'd come home from work he hadn't wanted to bore her with details of his day. He'd wanted to lose himself in the sweetness of her body. His role had been to protect her, to provide for her, and he'd been determined to do so to the best of his ability. But instead of appreciating his efforts, she had been so unhappy that she had walked out on him.

Women were totally incomprehensible, he decided bitterly. It seemed that whatever he did he couldn't win, but children were a different matter. His feelings for his son were uncomplicated. He loved him unreservedly and he was determined not to make the same mistakes his own father had. Jean-Claude would never have reason to doubt his love, he vowed fiercely. According to Emily, he had been a useless husband but he was going to be the best father ever.

He swung round and headed for the door of the nursery, pausing for a moment to glance back at her impatiently. 'Did Simone not give you the dress I bought you?'

'She did, but I told you I don't want anything from you.' Certainly not a dress he had requested his personal assistant to choose for her, Emily thought furiously. How insensitive could he get? 'I prefer to wear my own clothes but I don't suppose my cheap dress meets your exacting standards.'

'*Non,* you look like a slut,' he said coldly, and instantly could have cut off his tongue as she paled. Why the hell did he want to hurt her? Was it really because he hated the fact that the dress was more revealing than he was happy with? It had never bothered him when his previous lovers had paraded around in next to nothing but Emily was his woman, his wife and he wanted to lock her away from the world. He was no better than his barbaric ancestor, he acknowledged disgustedly, no better than his father. The thought shattered all his preconceived notions about himself.

'Our guests are already here,' he muttered, tearing his eyes from the dejected slump of her shoulders. Her head came up.

'Good, because the only clothes I possess are shorter and briefer and altogether more *sluttish,*' she told him fiercely. 'Not at all what your designer brigade friends are used to.' She would not give him the satisfaction of knowing his one vicious taunt had demolished her self-confidence, but as she stormed past him he gripped her arm.

'My friends have waited a long time to meet you and are under the impression that, together with Jean-Claude, we are one happy family. Let's not disillusion them,' he warned softly.

'Meaning what?' Emily demanded ungrammatically, and he paused at the top of the stairs to stare down at her.

'Meaning that tonight you will act the part of my adoring wife, blissfully happy that we are reunited.'

Why was he so eager to prove that their relationship was happy? Emily wondered with a frown. He was a fiercely proud man. Perhaps he couldn't bear the idea of his friends knowing that she had walked out on him. 'I'm afraid my acting ability's not that good,' she informed him coolly as she swept down the stairs in front of him and he laughed sardonically.

'Then improvise, *chérie,* like you did this afternoon. You were so adamant that you didn't want sex with me but I would never have guessed it from your wild response when you shared my shower. You're more talented than you think.'

Emily was still searching for a suitable retort when they reached the door of the salon and a tall, elegant blonde stepped forward to greet them.

'Emily, it's been a long time,' she murmured in the cool, faintly amused tone that Emily remembered so well, and her heart plummeted. Robyn was as stunning as ever in sumptuous, floor-length black velvet that was moulded to her body like a second skin, and Emily was immediately conscious of her cheap, brightly coloured dress. What on earth had induced her stupid spurt of rebellion? she wondered dismally. She should have worn the dress Luc had bought her, but it was certainly too late to change now and the familiar sick nervousness tied her stomach in knots as she braced herself to meet his guests. 'Everyone's dying to meet the mysterious Madame Vaillon,' Robyn murmured, so softly that only Emily heard. 'Let's hope they're not disappointed.'

As Luc's friends instantly surrounded him Emily felt as though she were invisible and hung back as he proudly introduced his son. Of course Jean-Claude was adorable, she acknowledged ruefully, and, far from being upset by the attention, he was lapping it up but as she slunk into a corner Luc turned and held out his hand.

'I'd like to introduce my wife, Emily,' he said, his burning gaze searing her as his eyes settled on her face and he lifted her hand to his lips. 'As you can see, I am doubly blessed to have such a beautiful mother for my son.'

Never mind her acting ability, Emily thought frantically, her cheeks burning as he pressed his mouth against her hand. He was surely in line to win an Oscar, but even the knowledge that it was all pretence did not stop her heart from pounding, especially when his lips found the pulse that jerked unevenly in her wrist. She could almost believe that the flare of warmth in his eyes was real and she trembled when, instead of releasing her, his lips travelled along her arm to caress the vein that throbbed in the crease of her elbow joint. His friends would be left in no doubt of his devotion to her but only she knew it wasn't real.

As an ice-breaker, Jean-Claude's presence was far more effective than the finest champagne and her initial awkwardness was forgotten as conversation with Luc's guests revolved around sleepless nights and teething gel. Far from being the social climbing business associates that she remembered from their life in Chelsea, these people were evidently Luc's trusted friends, people he had grown up with and who now had families of their own. Gradually Emily began to relax.

'I adore Jean-Claude's little suit,' commented a pretty, vivacious woman from the group that had circled round to admire the baby. Nadine Trouvier was the wife of Luc's closest friend, Marc. The mother of two small girls, she owned a successful babywear shop in Orléans and had confided that she was about to open another in Paris. 'Where did you buy it?' she queried interestedly. 'It's exquisitely made, especially the hand smocking at the front. Without wanting to appear rude, it must have cost a fortune. Only the best for your son, hmm, Luc?'

'*Naturellement,*' he replied coolly, but Emily knew from

the way his eyes had narrowed that he was speculating on how she had been able to afford expensive baby clothes when she had little money.

'Actually, I made it,' she informed Nadine cheerfully. 'I lived…in Spain for a while.' She felt Luc stiffen but continued, 'And I fell in love with the incredible baby clothes sold in the markets. But I found that although they looked beautiful, they were impractical and the fabric was often stiff and uncomfortable. I searched for better fabrics and redesigned the very formal baby clothes that the Spanish love so that they were more wearable. See…' She showed Nadine. 'The collar of Jean-Claude's suit is detachable and the suit fastens underneath so that dressing him is easier. He doesn't have a lot of patience for lying still while I dress him,' she added with a rueful smile, and Nadine nodded eagerly.

'I had the same trouble with my own two. Emily, this is wonderful. Do you have many other designs?' Nadine demanded enthusiastically. 'Have you ever thought about making them to sell? I would be very interested in stocking this sort of thing in my shops.'

'Well, I'd started up a little business in Spain,' Emily admitted, refusing to meet Luc's gaze. 'My friend runs a cookery school, predominantly for middle-aged ladies who bought my clothes for their grandchildren. They proved so popular that I started to receive orders from around the world. I employed a few girls from the village to help with the sewing and now it's a thriving little business. Fortunately Laura is overseeing things while…' She hesitated, about to say while she was away, but the darkness of Luc's expression made her change to, 'At the moment. It was good to be able to earn money doing something I enjoyed and at the same time care for Jean-Claude. Sewing was the only thing I was any good at when I was younger.'

'Along with riding,' Luc interrupted, taking her by surprise as he strolled across the room and slipped his arm around her waist. 'My wife is an excellent horsewoman,' he proudly told his guests. 'She's quite fearless aren't you, *chérie?*' His smile had the sickly sweet quality of an old movie but everyone seemed to be taken in by his attentiveness and no doubt believed they shared a marriage made in heaven, Emily thought grimly. Only she knew the truth, that Luc's loving looks had been a ploy to turn the conversation from her life in Spain without him. For some reason he wanted to project an image of a blissfully happy couple but she didn't know why and if she didn't stop smiling soon her jaw would surely crack!

'Seriously,' Nadine said, when Emily had handed Jean-Claude over to his nanny and they filed into the dining room, 'you'll have to persuade your husband to set up a workshop for you in the château. There's a ready market for the superb-quality hand-stitched clothes you can make. Parisian mothers will love them and I'm prepared to offer you an excellent deal if I can stock them in my shops. We'll save our discussion for another time,' Nadine added quietly as Robyn stared over at them, unable to disguise her annoyance for a few seconds before her tight smile slipped back into place. Emily smiled gratefully at the Frenchwoman, glad to have found an ally. She had a feeling she was going to need one.

It was late by the time the last of Luc's friends drove out of the gates of the château and the dull ache across Emily's temples had become a shaft of throbbing pain. Robyn was, of course, staying at the château and had joined her and Luc on the front steps to wave goodbye to the guests. Quite a cosy little threesome, Emily brooded darkly as she trailed across the entrance hall after her husband. Robyn had barely spoken to her all evening and that suited her fine. They had nothing to say to each other. She wasn't blind. She had noted the furtive, almost desperate glances Robyn had given Luc throughout dinner, but curiously he hadn't responded and had seemed oblivious to his personal assistant's attempts to gain his attention. Emily was ready to believe he had been telling the truth when he had denied an affair with Robyn, ready to believe that Robyn had lied to her, but it didn't change anything, she thought sadly. It didn't mean that Luc loved her.

'I'm going to bed,' she announced bluntly as she reached the sweeping staircase and viewed it with dismay. There suddenly seemed to be an awful lot of stairs and she was shocked by how tired and drained she felt. It felt like weeks since she had begun the day at San Antonia.

'Emily, are you all right, *ma petite?* You look so pale.' Luc murmured his concern and for a brief, mad moment she imagined that they were the happy couple he had been so desperate to portray. In the fantasy, he would sweep her into his arms and carry her up the long staircase to that vast bed where he would make love to her with such tender passion that she would never want him to stop. That wickedly sensual mouth would explore every inch of her body, coax each nerve ending to vibrant, throbbing life until, utterly satiated, they would fall asleep in each other's arms.

'Let me help you, *chérie.*' His voice broke through the sensual haze that enveloped her and for a moment she forgot that they were at war, forgot that the game of happy families had been for his guests' benefit only. She smiled at him, her heart in her eyes, and heard him inhale sharply before Robyn's sharp tones shattered the spell.

'If you could just spare me five minutes to run through this

GET FREE BOOKS and FREE GIFTS WHEN YOU PLAY THE...

7 Lucky

Just scratch off the silver box with a coin. Then check below to see the gifts you get!

SLOT MACHINE GAME!

YES! I have scratched off the silver box. Please send me the 2 free Harlequin Presents® books and 2 free gifts for which I qualify. I understand I am under no obligation to purchase any books, as explained on the back of this card.

306 HDL EF37   **106 HDL EF4Y**

FIRST NAME

LAST NAME

ADDRESS

APT.#

CITY

STATE/PROV.

ZIP/POSTAL CODE

report,' she murmured, 'it's urgent. I'm sure Emily understands the importance of heading a multimillion-pound company.'

'Can't it wait until morning?' Luc replied tersely, and Robyn edged closer, her hand resting lightly on his sleeve. For the life of her she would not fight with Robyn over her husband like a couple of curs over a bone, Emily thought savagely, and she moved abruptly away from him.

'I promise not to keep him for too long,' Robyn assured her sweetly, and Emily discovered she possessed acting skills she hadn't known she had as she flicked them a disdainful glance.

'Have him for as long as you like,' she murmured in a tone that screamed her bored indifference. 'I don't want him.' With that she marched up the stairs, aware of Luc's furious gaze burning like a laser between her shoulder blades. Robyn was welcome to him, she told herself sternly. She had already consigned their marriage to the graveyard of broken dreams. She had Jean-Claude and now, it seemed, a chance to build a career that would give her not just financial independence but also a feeling of self-worth.

As she was about to place her foot on the next step, it disappeared. The walls tilted alarmingly and she found herself lifted and held tight against the uncompromising solidity of Luc's chest. 'You are perilously close to having me demonstrate here and now just how little you want me, *chérie,*' he breathed against her ear.

The rigid muscles of his arms around her warned of his simmering anger, but Emily was aware of other, more subtle sensations—the warmth that emanated from him and the musky scent of his aftershave that did strange things to her insides. She fought the longing to press her face against the tanned column of his throat where he had removed his tie and unfastened the top few buttons of his shirt. Being held this close to his chest drugged her senses and dulled her wits when she needed them to be razor sharp.

'An interesting idea, but Robyn might not approve,' she murmured with a coolness that masked her inner turmoil.

'Damn Robyn!'

'For once I couldn't agree with you more.' He was nearing the master bedroom and a wave of panic assailed her so that she wriggled wildly until he was forced to set her down. 'I want to check on Jean-Claude,' she whispered, brushing past him into the nursery. She crept over to the cot and as she stared down at her son's innocent, sleeping form, Emily's resolve hardened.

'I want to be free to live my own life,' she whispered fiercely. 'I can't stay here as your prisoner, waiting for the day Jean-Claude no longer needs me. There are things I want to do.'

'Such as set up your own business?' he suggested scathingly, and she rounded on him angrily.

'Yes, damn it. What's so wrong with that?' Her voice had risen along with her anger. Jean-Claude stirred, and with an oath Luc caught hold of her arm and steered her through the connecting door to the master bedroom.

'Your role is here, as Jean-Claude's mother and my wife,' he told her as he swung her round to face him. 'Isn't that enough? *Mon Dieu,* it's not as if we need the money.'

'Sometimes I think you're trapped in a time warp,' Emily ground out, her frustration tangible. 'It's not about money. I've finally found something I'm good at after a lifetime spent being the untalented daughter and the unsuitable wife. I want the chance to make my mark on the world—a tiny mark, I know,' she added self-deprecatingly, 'but as Jean-Claude grows older I want him to be proud of me.'

'And you think that will happen if you are completely absorbed in your career?'

'Obviously he will always come first,' Emily muttered, the resoluteness of Luc's expression warning her that this conversation was going nowhere, 'but I should have known you wouldn't approve. You never wanted me to work or have the chance of meeting people my own age, even before I was pregnant. Look what happened when I got a job at Oscar's.'

'You were waiting tables,' Luc exploded.

'At one of London's top restaurants. It was hardly a greasy burger bar.'

'It was still not a suitable occupation for my wife.'

'And didn't you make your feelings felt?' she muttered sullenly. 'I still can't believe you marched in there while I was on duty and carried me out over your shoulder. You totally humiliated me,' she added, recalling the furious row that had followed his high-handedness. Their furious argument had ended as they always had, with her absolute capitulation in bed. She groaned inwardly at the shaming memory of her weakness where he was concerned. 'Laura said you were a control freak,' she told him bitterly, and his eyebrows rose quizzically.

'The same Laura who persuaded you to hide away in Spain I assume. You must remind me to thank her if I ever see her,' he drawled sarcastically. 'Let's just hope she doesn't take up a career in marriage guidance.'

'Its all academic now, anyway,' Emily said wearily. It had been the longest day of her life and she just wanted to go to bed, alone. 'A few weeks after you forced me to give up my job, I discovered I was pregnant and the rest, as they say, is history.'

Luc raked a hand through his hair as he paced the bedroom floor. His slightly dishevelled state gave him a raffish charm that Emily found irresistible.

'I accept that I was not there for you as much as I should have been during your pregnancy.' The admission seemed to have been dragged from him and Emily gave a bitter laugh.

'You weren't there, full stop. Suddenly your business interests in New York, Rome and every other part of the globe were far more important than spending time with me.'

'There were reasons…'

'Number one being that you were revolted by my body as my pregnancy progressed.'

'*Sacré bleu,* that is absolutely not true.' Luc's voice hissed between his teeth like a geyser letting off steam. 'I don't know how you could say such a thing.'

'It is true,' Emily insisted miserably. 'My mother explained that some men find pregnancy a turn-off. She told me not to worry and assured me things would return to normal after the baby was born, but she was unaware that our marriage wasn't normal to begin with.'

'Why, because I was busy at work and didn't give you enough attention?' Luc suggested angrily. 'I thought the world had gone mad in those months before you left,' he told her grimly. 'There were problems within the company, the suspicion of fraud at a high level, which meant I couldn't delegate to anyone but a few trusted staff. The timing could not have been worse.' he said thickly. 'I was worried about you. You were so young to be facing the rigours of childbirth and the constant sickness left you drained. I used to look at you sometimes and feel overwhelmed with guilt. I should never have married you,' he finished huskily. 'I should have let you remain innocent and carefree with your horses.'

For a moment Emily thought her heart had actually cracked open as pain tore through her. Luc had finally admitted that he believed their marriage had been a mistake and she felt numb with misery. 'Yes, well, it's a pity for both of us that you didn't, but even if our marriage is something we both regret, I could never regret having Jean-Claude, which you patently did. You can't blame me for believing that you didn't want him when you rejected him.'

The faint glow of the candles cast shadows around the room and Luc's face looked as if it had been carved from marble, his eyes glinting like molten steel as he glared at her. 'When did you ever give me the choice?'

'The day I brought him to see you.'

His eyes narrowed, his tension palpable. 'You're lying!'

'Why would I?' she snapped impatiently. 'It was December, bitterly cold, and Jean-Claude was about six weeks old. It had taken me a while to get over his birth,' she continued falteringly when he simply stared at her in a silence that spoke volumes. 'I went to the penthouse. I thought, even if you weren't there, I could show Jean-Claude off to your housekeeper, Mrs Patterson, but it was Robyn who opened the door.'

She broke off, recalling the unmistakable triumph in Robyn's voice as she explained that Luc was too busy to see her now, or any time in the foreseeable future. Robyn had stood in the doorway, tall and impossibly elegant, barring Emily's entrance to what had once been her home and uncaring that the freezing temperature outside was unsuitable for the baby.

'She told me what you've just admitted, that you thought our marriage was a mistake and you had no desire to be saddled with a child.'

In a flash Luc strode across the room and caught hold of her, bruising the tender flesh of her upper arms. 'This can't be true! I thought I was unshockable where you're concerned, but to stoop so low that you could accuse one of my most trusted aides, my sister-in-law, of deliberately engineering a split between us is too much to forgive, even for me, *chérie*. You disgust me,' he said savagely and she winced as his fingers gripped harder. 'Robyn was as concerned about your disappearance as I was.'

'Of course she was,' Emily muttered sardonically, wincing as his fingers bit into her skin. 'Luc, my arms. You're hurting me.' To her relief he released her immediately and she sank onto the edge of the bed as her legs buckled beneath the force of his fury.

'Why would she do such a thing?' he demanded in a low whisper that sounded like the rumble of a volcano about to erupt. 'She knew how desperate I was to see my child. Why would she try to keep me from him?'

'Because she wanted you for herself,' Emily said wearily, 'and still does. Presumably she feared that if you were as anxious to see Jean-Claude as you say you were, you might have been prepared to give our relationship another go. She really needn't have gone to so much trouble,' she snapped. 'It would be easier to raise the *Titanic* than resurrect our marriage.'

'I don't believe you,' Luc said, but this time there was a note of uncertainty in his voice and the hand that he raked through his hair was not quite steady.

'Then ask her.' Emily threw down the challenge. 'Because I swear to you, I'm telling the truth.'

CHAPTER SIX

HE WAS NOT a control freak!

Emily's accusation resounded in Luc's head as he stormed into his study and poured himself a liberal cognac. It was true he hadn't wanted her to work in the restaurant, but what husband would be happy to see his wife rushed off her feet until late at night? It had all been the fault of that damned chef whose vicious tongue had been feared among the other staff at Oscar's Diner. For reasons he could never understand, Emily had struck up a firm friendship with Laura Brent, although it was only now that he appreciated Ms Brent's role in Emily's disappearance.

Had she really been as unhappy in London as she had revealed tonight? His conscience nagged that it had been an incredibly busy and stressful time for him workwise and it was true they hadn't spent much leisure time together apart from those interminable dinner parties Robyn had organised. Perhaps she had been lonely, a young girl in a big city, but he had tried, he assured himself. How many times had he rejected the comfort of a hotel in favour of driving through the night just so that he could spend a few precious hours with her? And she had always been pleased to see him. Despite his best efforts to slide into bed without waking her, she had stirred and snuggled close, her hand straying a familiar path to wreak havoc on his self-control.

How the hell had it all gone so wrong? he wondered bleakly as he downed his drink and refilled the glass. He freely admitted he had been irritated by her unreasonable jealousy of Robyn, but he'd hoped the holiday would give them a chance to unwind and rediscover the joy they'd shared in the early days of their marriage. Instead, it had been an un-mitigated disaster.

Even now the sight of her paper-white face haunted him when he recalled the way she had slid to a crumpled heap at his feet. A virus, some unusual tropical disease she had picked up, would have been terrifying enough, but the realisation that it was history of the most tragic kind repeating itself had rendered him almost beside himself with fear. He hadn't been angry at the news of her pregnancy, he'd been scared witless at the thought of losing her. Even after she had sailed through the first few months safely, he had been unable to relax and as time had moved inexorably closer to her due date he had distanced himself, emotionally and physically, following a defence strategy learned from his childhood.

The damage he carried from his past was not Emily's fault, he conceded grimly, especially as he had never confided his fears to her, or the reasons for them. It was his fault he had failed her and now he was behaving no better than his father. He couldn't realistically hold her prisoner at the château. She was young and vibrant and wanted to live her life to the full, but the knowledge that she didn't want to live it with him hurt immeasurably, almost as much as her accu-sation that he had rejected her and his son soon after Jean-Claude's birth.

She had to be lying, he decided wearily, because the alternative was that the woman who had been his most trusted confidante for the last few years had deliberately deceived him. But in his heart there was no doubt where his loyalties lay.

Emily stood watching her sleeping son long after Luc had stormed from the nursery. Poor, innocent Jean-Claude, she thought sadly, caught up in the crossfire between the two people who loved him most. And Luc did love his son. She'd witnessed firsthand the mutual bond of adoration that had sprung between them from the moment he had lifted Jean-Claude into his arms.

Was it possible that Robyn had lied a year ago when she'd insisted that Luc wanted nothing to do with either his wife or child? Perhaps if Mrs Patterson had been there, Emily would have tried harder to enter the flat that was technically her own home. But there had been no sign of Luc's friendly housekeeper, no sign of Luc, and Robyn had appeared so self-assured, so stunningly beautiful compared to Emily's pale, sleep-deprived state, that she had been more than ready to believe her husband had chosen the ex-model over her.

With a sigh, Emily slid off the bed. The headache that had started during dinner had settled to a nagging sensation above her eyes. Usually she disliked taking painkillers but tonight she needed something to dull the ache around her heart. She'd noticed the medicine cabinet in the bathroom adjoining the master bedroom and quickly searched for a couple of painkillers before Luc found her. The last thing she wanted was for him to think she was preparing herself for a night of passion when she was utterly determined she would never share his room or bed again.

With that thought in mind she swallowed the painkillers, removed her make-up and freed her hair from its chignon so that it fell in a heavy swathe down her back, before making a swift exit. The room across the landing where she had asked Simone to transfer her clothes was smaller than the master bedroom but it was pleasant enough and she was so tired she doubted she would be awake long enough to admire the décor. Wearily she snapped on the light switch but the room remained in darkness, apart from the sliver of moonlight that streamed in between the crack in the curtains. She cursed as she stubbed her toe, but it was too late now to change the bulb, even if she knew where to find one. She closed the door and for good measure dragged the heavy dresser in front of it. Luc no doubt assumed that his *biddable* wife would be sleeping in his bedroom, but if he thought he could flit between her and his mistress, he was in for a shock.

'It's all right, *chérie,* I'm a willing captive. You don't need to barricade me in!'

A bolt of fear caused her to cry out, her heart pounding in her chest as she stared at the tall, menacing figure just visible in the doorway leading to the *en suite.* 'How did you get in here?' she demanded, her disbelief turning to a mixture of fury and embarrassment when she realised he had watched her struggle to pull the dresser across the door. 'You must have lost your way—your room's across the hall,' she added sweetly, striving for the brand of sarcasm he used with such deadly effect. 'And do you know where I can find a spare light bulb?'

Instead of replying, he strolled across the room and flicked on the bedside lamp so that the room was bathed in a gentle glow, his cold smile sending a frisson of apprehension along her spine as he held up the bulb he had removed from the ceiling light fitting. His silence unnerved her yet she could not drag her gaze from him. Tall, dark and devastatingly sexy, *he* unnerved her, she acknowledged wryly. Her tiredness seemed to have vanished and she felt strangely energised, every nerve ending tingling with a sense of expectation that refused to be quashed.

'I'm sure you have your reasons for snooping about in the dark, but I'm tired and not in the mood for playing games,' she told him shortly, and his jaw tightened.

'I'm not the one playing games and it's you who's in the wrong room. As my wife, you have certain duties to perform,' he reminded coolly, and the sheer arrogance of his statement fuelled her temper.

'I'm taking early retirement but I'm sure you'll have no problem filling the vacancy in your bedroom. As for performing, I did that this afternoon. You don't really think I enjoyed myself, do you?' she queried tightly, praying he wasn't remembering her eager capitulation in his arms.

'*Non, chérie,* I would never have guessed from your energetic response between the sheets that you hated every minute of making love with me,' he drawled, and her face flamed.

'Well, I did and I'm not planning an encore.' With the dresser wedged across the door and Luc barring her way to the bathroom she seemed to have reached stalemate and she gave an exasperated sigh. 'I would really appreciate being left in peace,' she said huskily. 'It's been a hell of a day.'

How did she manage to look so achingly fragile? Luc wondered savagely. Her air of vulnerability never ceased to affect him. Her eyes had darkened to the colour of midnight and appeared far too large for her pale, heart-shaped face. Her hair fell almost to her waist and he fought the urge to wind his fingers into the chestnut strands and pull her in. She was his woman, his *wife,* damn it, and he wanted her with a hunger that bordered on the obsessive, but she had tried to barricade herself out of his reach.

Was she afraid of him? The thought made him pause fractionally, but every instinct told him it was not fear that made her shrink from him. He knew her too well, recognised the fierce sexual tension that gripped her so that her pupils dilated and she was forced to moisten her lips with the tip of her tongue. She wanted him as badly as he wanted her, but convincing her of that fact was going to take more patience than he currently possessed.

'I am your husband, the man you agreed to love, honour and obey, if I remember the wording of the old service that *you* decided on. For ever, *chérie.* Until death us do part. Isn't that the promise we once made?'

'We also promised to stand by one another in sickness and in health, but you broke that one the minute you learned I was pregnant,' she said shortly, dragging her gaze from his hard-boned, handsome face.

'When I failed to give you enough attention?' he murmured silkily. 'Rest assured I won't make the same mistake again, *ma petite.* There will be no separate rooms, nothing to fuel gossip among the staff. Simone has already spent half the day transferring your belongings between rooms.'

At that Emily flung open the wardrobe, her temper heating to boiling point when she found it empty.

'You are my wife and you will share my bed,' he stated, and the implacable determination in his gaze was the last straw.

'Lucky me,' she quipped, striving for sarcasm to hide her trepidation as he shoved the dresser away from the door and headed in her direction. 'Did you ask Robyn why she kept quiet about my visit to the penthouse?' she demanded, unable to hide the hint of desperation in her voice as he suddenly pounced and scooped her into his arms, ignoring the blows she aimed at his chest with insulting indifference.

'I didn't need to. I already know you were lying.' His voice was so flat, so certain that her hands stilled and she stared into his face that was only inches from hers. 'I checked back in my diary,' he explained coolly. 'At the time you say you took Jean-Claude to the flat, I was in South Africa, partly on business but also to spend Christmas with friends who understood my desperation that I still had no knowledge about the whereabouts of my child.' His fingers tightened their grip and she winced as he kicked open his bedroom door and strode across to the huge, ornate bed. 'My housekeeper had gone to Yorkshire to visit family and Robyn flew from our meetings in Durban to stay with her parents in the States. The penthouse was shut up for the whole of December,' he told her hardily. 'There's a chance, I suppose, that you did go there, but why make up the rubbish about seeing Robyn? Why make her out to be a liar?'

'Why would I invent the story at all?' Emily defended herself as he threw her onto the bed with enough force that she bounced on the mattress. He shrugged, his indifference warning her that he was growing bored with the conversation.

'Perhaps because if you insist on leaving me, you'll have to fight a custody battle over Jean-Claude, and you think it would show you in a slightly better light if you said you had tried to contact me and allow me see my son?'

'I did go to the flat and I did see Robyn,' she yelled, dismay that he refused to believe her mingling with fear and a slow-building excitement as he began to unfasten his shirt. The room was illuminated by discreetly placed uplighters and dozens of thick church candles grouped on the fireplace, their flickering flames casting shadows on the walls. It was intensely romantic, a room designed for lovers, but there was nothing loving about the hardness of Luc's expression and the gleam in his grey eyes warned of his determination to fulfil his rights.

'I'm not a liar,' she said thickly, despising the way her voice had softened, the way her eyes fixed of their own accord on his bare chest. In the candlelight his skin gleamed like bronze and she clenched her fingers into fists so that she could not give in to the temptation to run her hands through the covering of wiry black hairs that arrowed down from his chest and disappeared beneath the waistband of his trousers.

'Do you want me to make love to you tonight, *ma chérie?*' he murmured softly.

'I'd rather have all my teeth extracted without an anaesthetic.'

'Then you are a liar.' It was his arrogance, the supreme self-confidence of his smile that set her teeth on edge. His hands moved to the zip of his trousers and she closed her eyes on a wave of despair as they hit the floor, closely followed by his underwear. Her breath snagged in her throat when he had to tug his silk boxers over the rigid hardness of his arousal.

Dear God, he was gorgeous she thought numbly. Earlier, in the shower, she had been so caught up with the exquisite sensations he had been arousing in her that she hadn't had time to study him properly. Now he was standing before her, his stance almost indolent, unhurried, and she was able to appreciate the full throbbing power of his erection. She should escape now, before it was too late, but instead her body quivered, betraying the primitive need that pinned her to the bed with a force she was unable to fight. It was only when he reached out a hand and threaded it through her hair that her instinct for self-preservation kicked in and she tried to scrabble off the bed, only to be lifted and deposited back on the mattress as if she were a rag doll.

'You had what you wanted this afternoon,' she muttered, although speech was difficult with her face pressed against his chest. Already she could feel herself weakening, molten heat flooding through her as the scent of him, a subtle blend of his exotic aftershave and male pheromones, assailed her senses.

'I want more.' His lips feathered along the line of her jaw and moved up to hover at the corner of her mouth, tantalisingly close so that it was all she could do not to close the gap and feel the full force of his kiss.

'But why me?' The words escaped as a wail of despair. 'You don't even like me and you certainly don't trust me,' she whispered on a note of pain. 'Isn't Robyn enough for you?' He had vehemently denied a relationship with his PA but all her old doubts had resurfaced with the knowledge that he believed Robyn's word over hers.

He ignored her, but his mouth settled on hers in an evocative caress that stunned her with its gentleness. She had braced herself for his fierce assault, had assembled her defences, but the sweetness of his kiss, the way he parted her lips with delicate precision so that his tongue could initiate an unhurried exploration, shattered her tenuous control over her emotions. This was Luc, the love of her life and the only man she had ever wanted. How could she deny him, how could she deny herself when her entire being was focused on assuaging this desperate, primal need for her mate?

She was unaware that his hands had slid beneath her hair

to unfasten the halter neck of her dress until he eased back a fraction and unpeeled the fabric from her breasts, leaving them exposed to his hungry gaze.

'Exquisite,' he breathed, his accent suddenly very pronounced, so innately sensual that she shivered and tiny goosebumps prickled her skin. 'I have never forgotten the scent of you, the feel of your skin like satin beneath my fingers. You are in here,' he whispered, frustration at his own weakness evident in his tone as he held her hand against his heart, 'and I can't seem to evict you, however hard I try.'

He didn't trust her, he refused to believe her story about going to the penthouse and he certainly did not love her, but right now Emily didn't care. He overwhelmed her senses, trampled on her pride so that all that was left was desire, piercing her soul and making every nerve ending zing with expectation. She drew a sharp breath as his hands slid down to cup her breasts, his thumb pads brushing across her nipples until they hardened into throbbing peaks that begged for his total possession. Slowly he lowered his head and she murmured low in her throat when his lips closed around first one peak and then the other, drawing it fully into his mouth as he suckled her. Sensation seared her, so that she arched her back to offer him unfettered access to her breasts but already his hands were sliding lower, tugging her dress over her hips while she knelt on the bed.

She gasped as he stroked the sensitive flesh of her inner thighs but was beyond any idea of rejecting him when he hooked his fingers into the waistband of her underwear and drew the scrap of lace down to her knees. Only then did he push her gently so that she fell against the pillows and he swiftly stripped her completely before coming down beside her, his body warm and male and urgently aroused. She wanted to say something, to tell him once more that she hadn't been lying about taking Jean-Claude to him, but her words were lost beneath the pressure of his mouth as he took her in a slow, sensual caress that drugged her senses and drove everything but the man and the moment from her mind.

When he dipped his hand between her thighs she parted them willingly, trembling as he stroked the sensitive nub he had revealed before he slid his fingers in deep to explore her intimately. She was ready for him, slick and wet, and she heard him groan low in his throat as her fingers strayed down over his hips to hesitantly touch the throbbing hardness of his arousal that pushed insistently against her belly. His hair-roughened thighs were abrasive against the softness of hers as he moved over her, his hands beneath her bottom lifting her so that she was angled to his satisfaction. He entered her, slowly, taking his time so that her muscles stretched to accommodate him. He filled her and she gasped as he began to move, sensation building on sensation, his rhythmic thrusts sending her higher every time he drove into her. Suddenly she was impatient, desperate to reach the pinnacle that she knew was ahead, and she wrapped her legs around him, urging him on, her pleasure mounting with the increasing speed of his movements.

Just when she thought she could take no more, her body splintered and she cried out as wave after pleasurable wave dragged her under, leaving her boneless and utterly spent. He was mere seconds after her and she heard him shout her name, his voice harsh as if it had been dragged from the depths of his soul, before he relaxed and she gloried in the weight of him pressing her into the mattress.

'You see, that wasn't so bad, was it, *ma petite?*'

On the edge of sleep, the unmistakable note of triumph in

his voice commanded her attention and her eyes flew open, sick humiliation filling her. Of course he sounded triumphant when she had made it so easy for him. Once again her defences had crumbled at the first touch of his hands on her skin. It wasn't bad, it was terrible, and she cringed away from the warmth of his body that even now had the power to arouse her.

'Are you hoping for a mark out of ten for technical ability, or simply waiting for a round of applause?' she demanded coolly as she sat up and dragged the huge silk-covered bolster into the centre of the bed. 'It wasn't that bad, but it wasn't that good either, and if it's all the same to you, I'd rather not repeat the experience.' With that she dived beneath the covers, hiding her hot face and praying that he wouldn't touch her because she would surely crack.

'Think very carefully, *chérie,* before you put a barricade between us,' he warned softly, 'because, I promise you, *I* won't be the one to remove it.'

'Excellent. Then I should get a good night's sleep without the fear of your hands straying into my side of the bed. Goodnight,' she added stiffly into the silence, and ground her teeth in impotent fury as he gave a low chuckle.

'*Bonne nuit, mon ange.* Sleep well!'

Sunlight slanting across her face caused Emily to open her eyes and she frowned as she stared around at the unfamiliar surroundings. Not the whitewashed walls of the farmhouse but the opulent décor of the master bedroom at the Château Montiard, she noted, her memory returning with a vengeance. She turned her head sharply but the space on the other side of the bolster was empty. Her gaze travelled to the clock and shock saw her scramble from the bed and into the *en suite.*

How on earth had she slept until ten o'clock, and why hadn't anyone woken her? Her thoughts turned immediately to Jean-Claude and she prayed he was happy with Liz. Her first opportunity to impress Luc with her maternal skills had got off to a bad start.

She showered in record time, wincing as ill-used muscles made themselves known. Her cheeks flooded with colour at the memory of just how she had exercised them. What madness had turned her into a wanton creature in Luc's arms last night? She had no one to blame but herself because he hadn't forced her. His methods of persuasion had been a far more subtle incitement of her senses that had left her begging for his possession.

A scant glance through her wardrobe revealed she had nothing suitable to wear for her role as the lady of the château and an imp of devilment saw her slip into faded denim pedal pushers that clung to her hips like a second skin and a bubble-gum-pink T-shirt with the slogan LITTLE MISS NAUGHTY emblazoned across the front. Elegant it wasn't, she conceded with a grin as she caught her hair into a ponytail and headed for the stairs, but her outfit was fun and funky and if Luc disapproved, too bad!

'Where's Jean-Claude?' she asked hesitantly, her bravado slinking away beneath Luc's cool stare as she crept into the dining room, to find no sign of her son or his nanny.

'Liz has taken him for a walk in the garden. He was growing impatient,' Luc added pointedly, and she blushed.

'I can't believe I overslept like that. Usually I'm awake at dawn.'

'Aha.' From his tone he patently believed she never woke up before lunchtime and her face tightened. She had spent the first six months of their son's life waking up every four hours to feed him because he was such a demanding baby. It was only in the last few weeks that she had persuaded Jean-Claude to sleep through the night and her body clock was frantically trying to make up for lost time.

'You've obviously never paced the floor at three in the morning trying to pacify a baby with colic,' she snapped, and he surveyed her steadily over the top of his newspaper.

'No, I was never given the chance.'

Hostilities had been resumed, she realised as she took her place at the table and smiled gratefully at Simone who placed a cup of steaming coffee in front of her.

'There's bread and croissants, or Sylvie will happily cook you something,' Luc murmured, and she quickly shook her head, her stomach rebelling at the idea of food.

'Coffee will be fine.'

'You must eat,' he argued, and then paused. 'Although perhaps not too much or you might actually burst out of your clothes, and they leave little to the imagination as it is.' His lips twitched as his gaze settled on the slogan across her chest and to her horror her breasts immediately swelled so that her nipples were prominently displayed beneath the thin cotton. 'And my imagination is in overdrive,' he commented dulcetly, to which there was no reply she could utter in polite company.

The silence stretched between them, so intense that the ticking of the clock seemed to reverberate around the room. 'Um, is there a spare car that I could borrow?' she asked at last, and he glanced at her speculatively.

'I'm afraid not,' he replied pleasantly, but she didn't trust his smile. He reminded her of an alligator, slumberous and watchful in the seconds before it snapped its great jaws around its unsuspecting prey. 'Where do you need to go? Everything you or Jean-Claude could possibly need is here at the château.'

'I'd still like to go into the village, or visit the nearest town occasionally. If it makes you happy, I'll leave Jean-Claude with his nanny,' she snapped impatiently, 'but you can't honestly expect to hold me prisoner at the château indefinitely.'

'I'm curious to understand why you're so anxious to leave,' he murmured, 'unless it has something to do with this mad idea of setting up your own business.'

His words stung and Emily felt her temper flare. He didn't think she could do it. Perhaps he didn't think she was clever enough to embark on a business venture but she was determined to prove otherwise.

'I'd certainly like to start looking for a workshop or some sort of premises where I can work. It doesn't need to be anywhere special,' she continued as he frowned, 'but big enough for a couple of cutting tables and sewing machines.'

'You're definitely going ahead, then?' he said shortly. 'Let's hope Jean-Claude is not unsettled when you abandon him.'

'I have no intention of abandoning him!' Emily jumped up furiously and scooted round to his side of the table. 'Anything I take on will fit around his routine. I've told you, he'll always come first.'

'In that case, shouldn't you concentrate you efforts on settling into the château so that the three of us can spend time together as a family?' he asked, his voice suddenly as soft as velvet. She swallowed at the lambent warmth in his eyes. In his faded jeans and a fine knit black sweater he looked deliciously sexy and she fought to restrain a shiver of pure pleasure that the sight of him induced.

'Aren't you going to work? I'm sure there must be something urgent on the other side of the world that needs your attention.'

'I told you, I'm learning to delegate,' he replied lazily. 'Having just been united with my son, I'm hardly likely to want to leave him—or his mother,' he added softly, and her stomach lurched.

'You're just saying that to…to get round me,' she muttered awkwardly, but could put up no resistance when he caught her hand and tugged her onto his knee.

'You're quite right. I intend to do my best to make you happy here.' His mouth hovered above hers and she closed her eyes to ward off temptation while her brain tried to assimilate his astounding statement. She couldn't let him kiss her, not when she needed to be on her guard against him, but somehow he had crept past her defences and she gave a little gasp when his lips brushed gently over hers. It was the lightest caress but it immediately made her want more and she lifted her lashes to find him staring down at her a curiously intent expression in his grey eyes.

'Why…why do you want to make me happy?' she asked huskily. 'We despise and mistrust each other. Why sentence us to remain in a loveless marriage?'

'I wouldn't describe our marriage as loveless, *chérie,*' he said quietly and for a brief, awesome moment her heart soared. What was he saying—that he loved her? 'We both adore Jean-Claude. For the sake of our son, I think we should try to put the past behind us and repair the cracks in our marriage. He deserves a stable and happy childhood, loved and cared for by both his parents.'

'For cracks read Grand Canyon,' Emily replied thickly when she could trust herself to speak. Of course he didn't love her. He'd only gone to the trouble of tracking her down because he had wanted to find his son. 'Naturally the only reason for us to stay together is for Jean-Claude's sake, but I'm not convinced it'll work. There's too much bitterness, on both sides,' she finished sadly.

'But we could try? Please, *chérie.*' He had lowered his head again and she knew she should turn her head to evade his mouth. Instead, she could not help but lean forward to close the gap between them, a soft moan escaping her when he captured her lips.

He took it slowly, as if he wanted to savour the moment and by the time his tongue dipped between her lips she was helpless to resist, curving her arms around his neck to draw him closer. She felt his hand slide beneath her hair, angling her head to his satisfaction as he deepened the kiss, the slide of his tongue sweetly erotic and deliciously intimate.

'You see, *ma petite,*' he whispered against her throat when at last he lifted his head, 'it's not over between us, it never could be. We owe it to ourselves, not just Jean-Claude, to call a truce.'

Wordlessly Emily nodded, her heart too full to speak. He didn't just want her at the château for Jean-Claude; it seemed that he really wanted their marriage to work, and hope filled her. She was prepared to meet him halfway.

'So, no more talk about setting up a business, hmm?' His words sent alarm bells ringing in her head. 'We need to devote all our time to each other and, of course, our son.'

'Luc…' She bit back her frustration as Liz carried Jean-Claude in from the garden and the baby's face lit up as he spied his father.

'Papa,' he shouted, justifiably proud of the second word he had mastered, and Emily turned her head away in despair. Luc had said he wanted to give their marriage another chance, and not just for the sake of their son. The news should have filled her with joy, it was more than she had ever hoped for, but it seemed that Luc didn't want an equal relationship—he wanted to own her body and soul. Could she do it? she wondered fearfully. Could she forget her dreams of combining a career with motherhood and make her role as Luc's wife the most important thing in her life?

'It's not over between us,' he had murmured, and she could not deny the truth. He was more important to her than a career and she would gladly sacrifice everything if only he would care for her. She would make him love her, she vowed fiercely as she slipped from the room. He wasn't immune to her, his passion the previous night was proof of that. She would win his trust and with it his heart, and she could not suppress a surge of joyful anticipation as she ran up the stairs to remove the bolster from their bed.

CHAPTER SEVEN

'SABINE REALLY WAS extraordinarily beautiful, wasn't she?' Robyn's cool voice echoed through the hall and Emily's heart sank as she dragged her eyes from the portrait that hung over the stairs. Robyn was poised on the landing above, looking effortlessly chic and understated in white blouse and matching linen trousers whose superb cut screamed their exorbitant price tag. With her blond hair curling about her shoulders, she looked as though she was about to star in a soap powder commercial, Emily thought sourly, but Robyn wasn't whiter than white, she was a liar and it was agonising to think that Luc trusted her.

'She is—was,' she amended hesitantly, 'incredibly lovely, but who was she?'

Robyn's finely plucked brows arched in surprise. 'You mean you don't know? Sabine was Luc's wife, the first Madame Vaillon. I assumed he'd told you,' she added when Emily continued to stare at her in stunned silence, unable to disguise her acute shock.

'He's never mentioned that he was married before,' she admitted thickly, disbelief giving way to humiliation that Robyn was privy to secrets that she knew nothing about. She felt as though her heart had been ripped from her chest. Why had Luc never told her? His first wife had been breathtakingly beautiful, her haughty demeanour emphasising her suitability for the role of lady of the château, and Emily was aware that any comparison would find her seriously lacking. 'How did she die?' she whispered, fighting the wave of nausea that swept over her.

'Sabine Bressan was a model—the muse of a famous designer at one of the top French couture houses—who went on to have a successful career as an actress,' Robyn told her. 'Luc fell in love with her at first sight. He adored her and they were France's golden couple, which made her death all the more tragic.'

'What happened…?' Surely Sabine hadn't taken her own life like two other Vaillon wives before her?

'She suffered an ectopic pregnancy. I'm not sure if she even knew she was pregnant until she collapsed in agony while they were holidaying on a remote island off Thailand. By the time medical help arrived, it was too late. Sabine was dead and Luc was utterly distraught. I don't think he ever really got over it,' Robyn confided. 'He loved her so much and he swore he would never marry again.'

'But he married me,' Emily pointed out huskily and Robyn threw her a scornful look.

'Yes, but that was different. He had his reasons…' She paused fractionally before murmuring sympathetically, 'Oh, dear, I'm afraid I've said more than I should. I admit I was surprised when you turned up again. I would have thought you'd got the message by now.'

'What message? Luc brought me here, I didn't ask to come, and he wants us to give our marriage another chance.'

'Well he would say that, wouldn't he?' Robyn intoned

softly. 'He has his son to consider. He'd do anything for Jean-Claude including keeping you around until he's gathered proof of your unsuitability as a mother that will swing a custody hearing in his favour.'

'I wonder what sort of proof he was gathering last night?' Emily snapped, her simmering temper disguising the sickness she felt inside. The knives were well and truly out and she was beyond trying to maintain even basic civility with Robyn.

'I wouldn't bank on using sex to hang onto him. You tried it once before and it didn't work. Luc is a man of superlative tastes but I suppose even a connoisseur needs a bit of rough now and again.'

'Which is presumably when he turns to you.' She might be dying inside but she refused to go down without a fight, Emily vowed fiercely, pride her only defence against Robyn's poison. 'You deliberately kept quiet about my visit to the Chelsea penthouse, didn't you? What do you think Luc's reaction would be if he discovered that his ultra-efficient assistant had actively prevented him from meeting his son?'

'I think you'll have one hell of a job proving it,' Robyn replied coolly, a slight smile playing on her lips. 'Luc and I go back a long way. He trusts me. Can you say the same, Emily?'

There was no simple answer to that, except for the humiliating confession that, no, he did not, and Robyn's smile widened.

'I'm on my way to find Luc now. You'll have to excuse us but we've hours of work to get through. Where are you off to?' she queried, her gaze slithering over Emily's funky T-shirt. 'Kindergarten, by the look of it!'

Emily had to move before she gave in to the temptation to push the bitchy blonde down the stairs. She hurried upstairs, desperate to lock herself away while her mind assimilated this latest blow.

Of all the secrets Luc had kept from her, the fact that he had been married before was the most shattering, she acknowledged as she curled up into a ball in the middle of the bed. Was it the reason he had decided they should live in London after their marriage rather that at the château, which had been his home with the stunning Sabine? Surely every time he looked at her he compared her with his beautiful first wife. Did he wish that Sabine was here now or, God forbid, did he close his eyes when he made love to her and pretend she was his first wife?

The idea made her feel physically ill and she pushed her knuckle against her mouth to hold back her sobs. Suddenly his aloof attitude and the fact that he had never intimated in any way that he loved her made sense. How could he love her when he was still mourning the woman he had adored? Sabine was an impossible act to follow Emily recognised despairingly, and it seemed even more likely that Luc only tolerated her because she had provided him with his son.

With her face buried in her arms she was unaware that Luc had followed her into the bedroom until she felt the mattress dip and she jerked her head round to find him sitting next to her.

'*Mon Dieu,* Emily! What is it, *ma petite,* are you ill?'

'Yes, I'm ill, I'm sick to my stomach,' she flung at him as she scrubbed her eyes with her hand and noted the traces of mascara on her fingers. She had never learned to cry prettily. No wonder he was staring at her with such dismay when she must look even more of a mess than usual and the knowledge increased her anger. 'Get away from me,' she snarled, recoiling from him as he reached out to stroke her hair from her damp face. His frown deepened.

'What happened to the smiling woman who half an hour ago agreed to give our marriage another go?' he queried, patently bemused by her transformation into a screaming harridan. Her hurt exploded in temper.

'Sabine! Sabine happened. Robyn took great delight in explaining about your first wife,' she yelled at him. 'Do you have any idea what a fool I felt? I'm your wife, damn it, but even members of your staff know you better than I do.'

Luc had visibly paled at the mention of his first wife's name and now he stood and raked a hand through his hair. 'So I was married before. It's no big deal,' he said coolly, and she stared at him wildly, unable to stop the tears that streamed down her cheeks.

'No big deal! It changes everything,' she sobbed. 'I thought I was special, I thought that the fact you'd married me meant I was important to you.' All the memories she'd clung to of their wedding day and brief, glorious honeymoon in Paris were worthless. He'd done it all before. 'The only ray of hope I had for our relationship was that you had chosen me for your wife, but once again I'm second best. I feel like the last prize in the raffle,' she whispered brokenly, 'the useless item that nobody wants.'

'Don't be so ridiculous,' Luc snapped, his grey eyes cold and so unemotional that she felt her heart splinter. 'Of course I want you.'

'Yes, for convenient sex when you happen to be around and haven't got anything better to do.'

'That's a lie.'

'Then why didn't you tell me about her? And don't tell me she slipped your mind,' she added bitterly. 'I've seen the painting of her. Hell, I could hardly miss it when it hangs in pride of place in the château. Robyn told me how much you loved her. Is that the reason you kept quiet? You thought I'd be jealous of her?'

'If it was, then I was right wasn't I?' he taunted, his eyes glittering as he stared at her tear-stained face. He was responsible for causing such devastation and the knowledge didn't make him feel good. He'd never meant to hurt her, he had wanted to protect her, but as usual she had completely misread his good intentions. 'Sabine died in terrible circumstances,' he said more quietly. 'It's not something I find easy to discuss and I could hardly reveal that it was her pregnancy that killed her when you'd just discovered you were carrying a child.'

'You should have told me,' Emily said stubbornly. His explanation made sense of sorts but she refused to be appeased. 'Why don't you just be honest and admit that you don't consider me important enough to share things with me? We've been married for two years but I hardly know you at all.'

'We've spent half that time apart, and whose fault was that?'

'Yours. It was your attitude that drove me away and nothing's changed, has it, Luc? You still don't regard our marriage as a partnership. As far as you're concerned, the only place I'm useful is in the bedroom.'

'If that's what you think then you'd better start earning your keep,' he growled savagely, the furious gleam in his eyes warning her she had pushed him too far.

'Luc, no.' He thwarted her attempt to scramble off the bed. 'Don't you dare touch me,' she yelled, her anger already turning to a fierce, unwanted excitement as he grabbed the hem of her T-shirt and yanked it up over her breasts. She tried to buck against him but his mouth came down on hers, his lips hard, hungry, demanding her response. She couldn't deny him, even now when she felt sick with betrayal that she had been the last to know about Sabine. When he kissed her, touched her she could forgive him anything, but the cost to her self-respect was too much to bear and tears slid from the corners of her eyes.

He must have felt them against his skin and lifted his head at last, his expression unfathomable as he stared down at her.

'Sabine was in the past. You are my wife now,' he told her as he rolled off her and pulled her T-shirt into place. 'For Jean-Claude's sake, if nothing else, I suggest you start acting the part.'

Pale rays of sunlight filtering through the curtains heralded another new dawn and Emily opened her eyes. Autumn was fast approaching. It was hard to believe she had been at the château for almost a month. Sometimes if felt as if she had been there for ever and she could barely remember a time without Luc.

It had not been an easy month, she acknowledged. In the days after she had learned about Sabine the atmosphere in the château had been fraught with tension. Luc had treated her with haughty disdain and she had refused to back down. He was in the wrong, she had reminded herself each night when she had hidden her face in the pillows and cried herself to sleep. He was the one who kept so much of his past a secret from her but until she felt that he trusted her there was no hope for their marriage.

The only glimmer of brightness was the fact that Robyn had left the château immediately after the upset over Sabine. Had Luc been angry that his PA had revealed Sabine's identity? she wondered. He had made no reference to either his first wife or Robyn, but in the last week she had noticed a distinct thaw in his attitude towards her. Perhaps the small birthday party they'd held for Jean-Claude had helped. It had been a joyous day as they'd celebrated his first year and Luc had been unable to disguise his pride as he'd showed off his son to his friends. Watching them together, father and son, Emily had felt a sharp stab of guilt that she had kept them apart. Luc loved Jean-Claude more than she had ever believed possible and his anger with her was understandable, but she had honestly never known he would care about their child so deeply and she had been unable to stifle a little pang of envy that Jean-Claude's place in Luc's heart was so secure.

With a heavy sigh she stared up at the billowing drapes that surrounded the bed, her breath catching when a familiar, indecently sexy voice sounded from the other side of the bolster.

'Why the sad sigh, *chérie*? Are you unhappy at the château?'

'No,' she admitted honestly, after a long pause during which she came to grips with the fact that Luc had not gone for his usual early morning ride but was lying only inches from her. 'Just confused.'

'*Oui.*'

The gentle understanding in his tone was her undoing and she bit down hard on her lip. The bolster seemed as insurmountable as the Berlin Wall had once been, a symbol of division that she had put in place and he had vowed he would never remove. He had stuck firmly to his promise and every night climbed into his side of the bed, bade her goodnight in a tone that licked over her like thick honey before he doused the lamp and within minutes appeared to be fast asleep.

Patently he was not tormented by the same aching desire that saw her toss and turn restlessly until the early hours. Even then her sleep was fractured by memories of his hands on her body, her dreams so wickedly erotic that she woke hot, flustered and desperate for him. It didn't help matters, she thought dourly, when every night he stripped in front of her, his lack of inhibitions all the more noticeable when she could not walk from the bathroom to the bed without her armour of a thick, all-concealing robe, her face burning as she leapt between the sheets with more haste than dignity.

Her one defence against her crumbling emotions was the knowledge that he only wanted her as his wife for the sake of their son. What other reason could there be? she wondered bitterly, when Sabine's exquisitely beautiful face taunted her every time she passed the portrait that took pride of place at the top of the stairs?

'Why didn't you go for a ride this morning?' she asked, desperate to break the silence between them. Her eyes widened as his face appeared over the bolster.

'I decided to wait for you. I thought you might like to join me.' With a night's shadowy growth on his jaw and his black hair ruffled from sleep, he reminded her of a pirate, his raffish charm too much for her to deal with first thing in the morning.

'Another time perhaps, although it was kind of you to ask,' she replied stiltedly, and his low chuckle filled her with longing to fling the bolster to the far corner of the bedroom. She loved the sound of his laughter, loved him, she accepted bleakly, but his sudden friendliness was an illusion, a trick, Robyn had assured her, to lull her into a false sense of security while he planned how to win custody of Jean-Claude.

'You'd be surprised at how kind I can be, *ma petite,*' he teased, 'and once you loved riding. In fact, you spent most of your time on Kasim.'

'It was a long time ago,' she whispered thickly as she

curled up into a ball beneath the bedcovers. It was stupid to cry over a horse, she told herself angrily as her mind relived the day Kasim had been sold, along with all the other horses from the stud at Heston Grange. A cost-cutting exercise her father had explained impatiently, unable to cope with her misery when he'd dropped the bombshell. He had never understood that she had turned to her horse for the affection she had never received at home.

Emily had fled to the stables, utterly distraught, and that was where Luc had later found her, pulling her firmly into his arms as he sank onto a hay bale and cradled her in his lap. His strong arms had offered comfort and she had clung to his wide shoulders as her tears had gradually subsided and she'd explained between hiccups that the deal had already been finalised. Kasim would be shipped out of the country by the end of the week, she had told him, her blue eyes filling once more. He had brushed an errant tear with his thumb pad before lowering his head to trace the same path with his lips.

She couldn't remember the exact moment the tenor of his caress changed, deepened to something that no longer offered comfort but instead revealed a burning passion that had been simmering beneath the surface. The first touch of his lips softly brushing over hers was a revelation and a fierce trembling started deep inside as his tongue traced the contours of her mouth. Hampered by her painful shyness, she'd had few boyfriends and her sexual experience was next to nothing, yet she knew instinctively what he wanted her to do and received a low murmur of approval when she tentatively parted her lips.

Suddenly all remnants of restraint were blown away as he crushed her to him, his mouth an instrument of sensual pleasure as he teased and coaxed her response in a blatant seduction of her senses. She had no thought to deny him, no thoughts of anything but him. Even her heartbreak over Kasim faded, obliterated by the myriad new sensations Luc was evoking within her. When he tipped back into the hay, taking her with him, she made no demur, her excitement reaching fever pitch when he unbuttoned her shirt, his hands warm and deliciously male on her midriff.

'You are exquisite, *ma belle*.' His voice stroked over her skin with the same dedication as his hands and she heard him inhale sharply as he eased her bra cup over one breast, his fingers finding its rosy nub and inciting it to swell until it throbbed unbearably. It was so new, so gloriously exciting, and far from feeling shy she was impatient for more, her hips arching beneath him and her soft cries of rapture filling the barn when he replaced his fingers with his mouth.

Who knew what might have happened if voices from the yard had not intruded on their sensual world? Even then, knowing they could be caught at any moment, she was loath to end her first experience of sexual pleasure, and it was Luc who gently eased away from her, sliding her bra back into place and refastening her shirt buttons when it became obvious that her hands were shaking too much to be of any use.

She had been like putty in his hands, Emily thought dismally, recalling his amused smile at her obvious disappointment that he was calling a halt to their love-making. She had been lost from the moment he'd first kissed her, a willing slave to his desires that more than matched her own. She had made the fatal mistake of confusing sexual attraction for love, because although he had undoubtedly fallen in lust, love had never entered his head or his heart.

'Come with me this morning?' His voice broke into her

thoughts, a welcome interruption from memories that still haunted her and she dragged her gaze from the sculpted beauty of his body as he strolled towards the *en suite* with a nonchalant disregard for his nakedness. 'We'll show Jean-Claude the horses and there's a quiet little mare who might be suitable for you.'

'So what do you think of Mimi?' Luc asked later as they stood in the yard, stroking the pretty bay mare the groom had led out from the stables. 'I admit she's getting on a bit but she's gentle and safe for you to ride.'

'Why don't you just order me a mobility chair and be done with it? I'm not a geriatric and I don't want to be safe,' Emily argued. She didn't want to seem ungrateful but neither did she want to plod around at the pace of a snail. 'Riding is all about thrills and excitement, the burst of adrenalin I used to feel when I took Kasim on a cross-country hack and we approached a five-foot hedge. It was brilliant,' she finished, her eyes shining, and Luc glanced at her, a curious expression on his face.

'It was dangerous,' he pointed out firmly. 'I know you're an excellent horsewoman, *chérie,* but I could never understand why your father allowed you to ride such a powerful animal.'

'Dad was always too wrapped up in running the estate to care about what I got up to,' Emily revealed cheerfully. 'I was a lasting disappointment to my parents. I should have been a boy, you see, an heir for Heston, but instead I was a fourth daughter and not even a pretty or talented one, like the other three. Nobody really cared as long as I kept out of the way,' she told him honestly, 'and I was more than happy to spend all my time with Kasim.'

Dear God, no wonder she suffered from such a crushing

lack of self-confidence, Luc thought grimly as he stared at
her upturned face. She had spent her life feeling second-rate
and she had needed someone to put her at the centre of their
world, not abandon her in the middle of a big city and
promptly leave her for weeks on end. Suddenly the reason for
her jealousy of Robyn became clear. She had felt threatened
by the older woman's sophistication, had perhaps compared
herself unfavourably, as she had done with her sisters. But he
had never once taken the time to reassure her that her inno-
cence and gentle beauty were the reasons he had fallen in love
with her. He had taken everything she had offered so freely
and given nothing in return, not his time, his exclusive attention, and perhaps most damaging of all, not his trust. He had
never found the courage to share his emotions. Was it any
wonder, then, that she had believed he didn't care?

'Well, I can see you're not impressed with Mimi,' he
murmured huskily, a mixture of guilt and confusion making his
throat raw. 'There is one other horse you might be interested in,'
he told her as she began to push Jean-Claude's buggy out of the
yard. 'The groom's just bringing him in from the paddock.'

Even from a distance the proud toss of the horse's head
was stomach-clenchingly familiar to Emily and she stiffened,
disbelief draining the colour from her face. 'Luc? It can't be
Kasim,' she whispered faintly, as the horse came nearer, his
hooves clattering on the tiled yard, his breath sounding in
loud snorts as he tugged on the lead rein so that it took all the
groom's strength to control him. 'Oh, my God!' She stumbled
forward, her eyes focused on Kasim, whose coat gleamed like
polished ebony in the sunlight, his tail twitching restlessly as
he stood, still trying to jerk the rein out of the groom's hand.

'Kasim, is it really you?' she asked wonderingly, and the
horse stopped tugging and lowered its head so that soulful

brown eyes were on a level with her own. For a moment she thought her heart would burst. She'd forgotten just how much he had meant to her, or rather not forgotten. She'd just buried the memory of him deep in her subconscious because losing him had hurt so much. Now she pushed her face into his neck, trying vainly to hold back the tears as he nuzzled her. 'My darling boy.' Her voice cracked with the emotions she couldn't hide and Luc swung away from the scene, feeling as though he was intruding. He wanted her to be happy, wanted it so much that he ached with it. She deserved so much more than he had ever given her but for so long he had failed her and her reaction to finding out about Sabine had brought home to him how cavalier he had been with her emotions.

'Oh, Luc, I can't believe he's real,' she whispered, and he blinked fiercely before turning to face her. He hadn't cried since he'd been a boy, since he'd looked down at his mother's shattered body and realised that his efforts to make her happy hadn't been enough. Failing the people he cared about the most was a regular feature in his life, he thought bleakly, and the utter joy on Emily's face pierced his soul. He didn't want to fail her.

'He must remember you. I haven't seen him this calm since he arrived,' he remarked diffidently. 'Can I take it that your tears are of happiness?'

'You know they are,' she said, scrubbing her eyes with her knuckles. Her smile caused a sharp pain in his chest. 'How did you find him? I thought he went abroad.'

'He did, and his new owner was loath to part with him, but fortunately I was able to persuade him to sell.' He did not add that it had taken all of his considerable charm and persuasive skills, not to mention a figure that was three times the value of the thoroughbred, before Sheik Hassan had agreed to a deal, but it was worth every penny to see the joy on Emily's face.

'But you can't have bought him for me?'

'Well, no one else can ride him, he's too damned feisty. Why shouldn't I buy him for you, *ma petite?*' he asked gently. 'I know how much you love him.'

'Oh, Luc!' Her heart was surely going to burst and with a cry she shot across the yard and threw herself against his chest, 'I love you. I mean…' She broke off, her eyes suddenly shadowed and her cheeks flooding with colour. 'Obviously not. What I meant was, I love what you've done…it was a lovely gesture.' She stepped away from him, her embarrassment painful to witness, and his heart clenched.

'You used to tell me all the time that you loved me,' he murmured quietly, and she refused to meet his gaze.

'Don't remind me. You must have found my eagerness very…tiresome.'

'*Non,*' he replied honestly, 'I found it very lovely. I liked to hear you say it.'

'But you couldn't say it to me.' She stepped back from him and blinked hard, desperate to banish her tears. She'd made enough of a fool of herself without suffering the humiliation of breaking down in front of him. 'It's all right,' she assured him when he reached out a hand to her. 'I know why, and I understand.' He couldn't tell her he loved her when his heart was with Sabine. 'Finding Kasim for me is the most wonderful thing you have ever done and I don't know how I can ever thank you.'

'Try,' he suggested softly, and the warmth of his gaze stunned her before his lips claimed hers, his kiss so sweetly evocative that she was forced to blink back the tears. He explored her mouth with tender passion and she closed her eyes as he dismantled her defences with an ease that should have appalled her. She'd missed him, she acknowledged honestly. For the past month she'd only been half-alive, waiting, longing for him to break down the barriers she'd erected against him, and now she was in his arms she never wanted to leave. The gentle probing of his tongue between her lips took the kiss to a new dimension and when she opened her mouth fully she heard him mutter something beneath his breath before he hauled her up against the solid wall of his chest, ready to crush any signs of resistance. But he need not have worried, she was all his.

'Your riding gear's in the tack room,' he murmured at last when he lifted his head to stare down at her, his body clenching as he studied her softly swollen lips. He was tempted to simply carry her off into the barn, lay her down on the sweet-smelling hay and make love to her until there could be no more doubts or mistrust between them. Instead, he reined in his desire and ignored the driving need that left a permanent ache in his guts. He had already blackmailed her into his bed once and although her resistance had been minimal, the next time he wanted her to come to him willingly, without duress and certainly not because she felt she owed him for her damned horse. 'Are you ready to try Kasim out?'

'Jean-Claude?' Emily glanced around, guilt assailing her as she belatedly remembered her son. Fortunately he was sitting in his buggy, seemingly fascinated by Kasim, and with excellent timing Liz walked across the yard.

There followed one of the most glorious hours of her life as she saddled up Kasim and joined Luc on his powerful palomino. Luc insisted they take it easy. Kasim was still un-settled by his new surroundings, he warned, and Emily was secretly surprised by the stallion's strength. She hadn't ridden for nearly two years, she consoled herself, and Kasim had always had a will of his own. It was one of the reasons she loved him, but her arms were aching by the time they returned to the stables.

'I want you to promise me you won't take him out alone,' Luc demanded as he helped her to dismount. Where she was hot and breathless from the ride, he didn't seem to have a hair out of place in tight jodhpurs that moulded his muscular thighs and a black lambswool jumper. 'In all honesty, Kasim is too big and powerful for you and if it wasn't for the fact that you love him so much, I would have bought you another horse.' He had spent the last hour on tenterhooks that she would be thrown. In his mind he could envisage her lying broken and bloodied on the ground and he was bitterly regretting his decision to buy the horse. How could he live with himself if she was hurt? It would be his fault.

'I'll soon get used to him again,' Emily began, and was subjected to a hard stare that brooked no argument.

'I mean it, Emily. You're only to ride him when either the groom or I can accompany you. Disobey me and I'll have no option but to sell him,' he finished grimly. 'I won't stand by and allow you to endanger your life.'

'What do I have to do to prove that I'm not a six-year-old?' she snapped in exasperation, her hands on her hips as she glared at him. His lips twitched.

'You've done that admirably already, *chérie,*' he murmured dulcetly, 'but I won't complain if you want to jog my memory!'

Their new-found harmony lasted the length of the walk back to the château. The Loire region of France was so beautiful, Emily mused as they strolled hand in hand along the lanes. Suddenly the countryside appeared even lusher and more vibrantly green, the cloudless sky an even denser shade of blue. It was as if her senses had gone into overdrive, the sound of birdsong sounding acutely sweet to her ears as her heart swelled with happiness. Luc had found Kasim for her. Not only that but he had hunted across several Middle Eastern states to find him and bring him to France. It had not been the action of a man who despised her. Perhaps he was starting to forgive her for keeping Jean-Claude from him and was even beginning to trust her. There was still a long way to go, she acknowledged as the memory of Sabine caused her heart to lurch. Maybe he would never love her the way he had his first wife, but suddenly the future seemed rosier than it had for a long while.

Life had a curious way of refusing to run to plan, she decided a few minutes later when they climbed the steps of the château and were met by Philippe.

'Monsieur Laroche is here to see you, Madame,' he murmured. 'The manager of the bank,' he added when she stared at him in obvious confusion. 'I asked him to wait in the salon.'

'Curious,' Luc murmured in her ear, his expression suddenly unfathomable, although the sexy smile had disappeared. 'Is it a social call, do you think, or business?'

'Business, I imagine,' Emily replied, horribly aware that her cheeks were flaming, proclaiming her guilt. How could she have forgotten the appointment she had requested Philippe to arrange with the bank manager to discuss her plans for setting up her own business? Without access to a car she had been forced to ask Monsieur Laroche to visit the château and had prayed that Luc would be busy in the nursery with Jean-Claude. In her excitement over Kasim the meeting had completely slipped her mind, and with a swift glance at Luc's furious face she pinned a smile on her lips and stepped into the salon to greet the dapper Frenchman.

'I hope you haven't been waiting long,' she murmured, aware of Luc's brooding presence by the fireplace as she offered Monsieur Laroche a seat. It was clear that Luc had no intention of awarding her privacy for her meeting and her baleful glare was met with a bland smile and a shrug of feigned misunderstanding that she wanted him to leave.

'Not at all. I fear I am a little early,' the bank manager replied gallantly. 'I understand that you want to discuss proposals for a business venture, Madame Vaillon,' he pressed on, valiantly trying to ignore the simmering tensions in the room. 'I am most impressed by the business plan you sent me.'

'Thank you,' Emily murmured, her eyes focused on Luc who had strolled over to join them and was leaning over to study her ideas for the babywear business. She wanted to snatch her folder from his hands and only a desire to spare Monsieur Laroche embarrassment forced her to retain a dignified silence. 'I'm certainly considering starting up my own business—'

'But not at the moment,' Luc finished for her, ignoring her gasp of indignation as he stood and offered his hand to the manager in a gesture that clearly indicated the meeting was at an end. 'My wife still has many things to consider before she goes ahead,' he murmured, the disturbing softness of his tone sending out a warning that he did not expect to be contradicted.

'I can't believe you just dismissed the poor man like that.' Emily rounded on him as soon as they were alone. 'It was so rude, especially when he had come all this way.'

'Whose fault is that?' Luc queried shortly, and her temper ignited.

'Certainly not mine. I couldn't drive into town because you won't lend me a car.'

'A decision that is obviously justified when you sneak behind my back at the first opportunity,' he said grimly. 'We discussed this and you knew I didn't want you to work.'

'Exactly, that's the reason I didn't want you to find out just yet. I'm fighting for my independence here, Luc,' she cried despairingly. 'I don't just mean financially. I need to be my own person. You can't simply expect me to live here in your country, in your grand house. I refuse to live my life as a poor imitation of the wife you lost,' she yelled at him, and then gasped and covered her mouth with her hands. It was too late, the damning words were out and she bit her lip as Luc's expression turned thunderous.

'Why do you insist on dragging other women into everything? My first wife bears no relation on our life now,' he growled, and Emily shook her head.

'She has everything to do with it. She haunts me constantly,' she admitted brokenly. 'Sabine was so incredibly beautiful. She must have been the ideal wife and mistress of the Château Montiard and I really can't compete. I don't understand how you could even bring yourself to sleep with me, you must have found me a poor substitute.'

'You understand nothing,' Luc flung at her savagely as he stormed over to the door and almost wrenched it off its hinges. 'But I'll tell you one thing, *chérie*. Sabine never installed a damned great bolster in our bed!'

CHAPTER EIGHT

IT WAS PAST midnight when Luc entered the bedroom and instantly disappeared into the *en suite*. Emily huddled beneath the covers, listening to the sounds of him showering and tried to banish the memories of the time he had dragged her beneath the spray with him. He emerged with a towel hitched round his waist, his hair still damp, and she noted the beads of moisture that clung to his chest hair, his skin gleaming in the soft glow from the bedside lamp. The powerful muscles of his abdomen rippled as he moved to sit on the edge of the bed. She squeezed her eyes shut, vainly trying to steady her breathing so that he would assume she was asleep.

'You're a hopeless actress, *ma petite,*' he drawled when the mattress dipped and she felt him slide between the sheets, although he kept to his side of the bed and the bolster remained firmly in place. 'I know you're awake, in the same way that I know how little sleep you get each night.'

'I don't know how, when you always fall asleep within minutes of your head touching the pillow,' Emily snapped, grateful that he had doused the lamp and her burning cheeks were hidden from his view.

'I've been awake, too. Sexual frustration's hell, isn't it, *chérie?*' he added softly.

'I wouldn't know,' she muttered, aiming for a bored tone but sounding annoyingly breathless. 'Goodnight.' She rolled onto her side to glare at the offending bolster and from the other side she heard him sigh.

'I owe you an apology. That last crack in the salon earlier was uncalled for.'

'But true,' Emily said miserably. 'Robyn told me how much you loved your first wife and how devastated you were by her death.'

'Did she?' Luc stared up at the canopy above the bed and gave a silent groan. He could hear the hurt in Emily's voice, the self-doubt. Would she feel any better if he revealed that he had fallen out of love with Sabine long before her tragic death? He had been afraid to tell Emily about his first marriage. It had not been the most edifying chapter of his life, he conceded grimly, and he had failed not only to be a good husband but also ultimately to save Sabine. Emily had hero-worshiped him, certainly at the beginning of their relationship, and he had liked the way she'd looked up to him. It had made him feel good about himself. Now she was looking at him as if she would never trust another word he said and he could hardly blame her. 'I didn't tell you about Sabine because she was in the past and not relevant to our future together. Obviously I was wrong,' he said heavily, 'and I wish you hadn't learned of her in the way that you did.'

'Robyn has always been determined to cause trouble between us,' Emily said wearily, but to her amazement Luc did not jump to his PA's defence.

'It seems so,' he admitted quietly, and she held her breath, not daring to hope that at last he was listening to her.

'Then ask her to leave. There must be plenty of other suitably qualified staff you could appoint as your personal assistant.'

'It's not that simple,' he replied heavily and she sat up and glared at him over the bolster.

'Why, because she was once married to your brother? You told me Yves died four years ago, and although I appreciate how devastating it must have been for Robyn, isn't it time she moved on with her life?' The silence stretched between them and she sighed. 'You said you wanted us to give our marriage another chance,' she reminded him huskily, 'but it's doomed to failure while Robyn remains between us—especially when you believe her word over mine every time,' she added bleakly. 'Does she have some kind of hold over you?' she demanded, her impatience growing at his continued lack of response.

'In a way.' His quiet confession shocked her to the core and she stared at him, wishing she could see his face properly, but his expression was shadowed in darkness. 'It's difficult to explain,' he added, wondering how he could possibly ask Emily to understand Robyn's fragile state of mind. She had adored Yves and his death had left her virtually suicidal with grief.

He had become her emotional prop, Luc acknowledged, and for the first time he realised how much Robyn must have resented losing his exclusive attention when he'd married Emily.

'How can you expect me to stay here with Jean-Claude when there are so many undercurrents that I don't understand?' Emily demanded angrily. 'Is it any wonder that I want to start up my own business and gain some independence, instead of being dragged into the murky underworld of secrets that you seem to inhabit?'

At that he sat up and snapped on the lamp so that she blinked at him owlishly. 'The Château Montiard is not a murky underworld,' he growled furiously. 'I thought you liked it here.'

'I do.' She gave up and flopped onto the pillows. She was talking and he was listening but somehow the messages were being scrambled and neither of them knew the code.

'I appreciate that you may feel cut off here but the city is not far away.'

'It is when you won't allow me the use of a car, and don't think I haven't guessed your reasons. You're afraid that I'll disappear with Jean-Claude, aren't you?'

'Trust has to be earned, *ma chérie*,' he said harshly, 'and going behind my back to discuss your business plans with the bank manager is hardly the way to impress me.'

Was it possible to beat a man senseless with a feather-filled bolster? Emily wondered. 'I've already explained that I wanted to research all the possibilities before I discussed them with you but I don't suppose you'd have listened even then, would you?'

'I don't know.' His control over his temper was more tenuous than she'd realised and his sudden shout of frustration made her jump, her eyes widening as she watched him rake his hand through his hair. She had never seen him so disquieted and despite everything her heart went out to him.

'I'm sorry,' she offered huskily. 'I know you don't understand and maybe even think I'm being ungrateful. From a financial point of view you can see no reason for me to work when you've provided me with such a wonderful place to live, but it's something I want to do, Luc, something for me. I never excelled at anything when I was younger,' she confided. 'My sisters were blessed with brains as well as beauty and I was always made to feel a failure. Designing and making clothes for Jean-Claude was a revelation. I'd finally found something I could do well and it developed into a successful little business in Spain. With Nadine Trouvier's help I know

I can start up again here. Nothing big. I'm not talking mass production,' she explained, leaning across the bolster in her eagerness to share her plans, 'but there is a place at the top end of the market for exclusive, hand-sewn babywear.'

'And it really means so much to you?' There was a new softness in his tone and his eyes were no longer hard bolts of steel but glinted with a curious emotion she couldn't define.

'As much as being reunited with Kasim,' she told him huskily and caught her lip between her teeth. 'You don't know how wonderful it was to see him again. I was…speechless.'

'I noticed,' he murmured dryly, 'possibly because it doesn't happen very often.'

'And then afterwards we argued and I never did thank you properly.' It was hard to think straight when he was looking at her like that. Her fingers itched to remove the bolster but something held her back. Sex between them would be as mind-blowing as always and she didn't doubt for a second that he was aware of the sparks of electricity that were practically arcing across the bed. Their physical compatibility had never been in doubt but where once she had settled for any small scraps of his attention he was willing to give, now it was not enough. She had grown up during their time apart, and although her love for him hadn't lessened, her self-respect had gone up several notches and she refused to let him destroy it.

Perhaps he understood the battle that was waging inside her better than she realized. Certainly he seemed to want to make it easy for her as he leaned across the bolster and cupped her face with his hand. 'Is it really so wrong to want to recapture what we once had?' he whispered, his mouth millimetres from hers so that she could feel the warmth of his breath on her skin. 'Is it really so hard to trust? You put in place this barricade to separate us and I swore I wouldn't breach it, however much I believe you want me to,' he said, his lips brushing as light as a feather against hers. 'But if you move it you'll find I'm more than willing to meet you halfway.'

It was more tempting than he could ever know, and for a few seconds her fingers curled around the bolster that had come to represent a wall as thick and unbreachable as the defences of the château. He kissed her with the pent-up hunger of a starving man, drawing her response as he used all the seductive skill at his disposal to part her lips and plunder the inner sweetness of her mouth. It was bliss and she couldn't bear for him to stop as heat coursed through her veins. It would be so simple to push the bolster out of the way and pull him down on top of her, wind her arms around his neck and hold him captive, but something held her back.

If she weren't the mother of his son, would she be here now? Would he have tried so hard to find her if Jean-Claude hadn't existed? She wanted to be wanted for herself, not because continuing with their marriage was in the best interests of their son. And what about Sabine? she thought despairingly. And Robyn? She accepted that he hadn't been unfaithful but she still mistrusted his emotional attachment to his personal assistant. Without trust, their love-making was reduced to a basic, primitive urge, devoid of any emotion.

She was breathless when at last he lifted his head, and the pulse at the base of her throat thudded unevenly. Her lips felt soft and swollen and she traced them with the tip of her tongue as if to capture the taste of him while he watched her through hooded eyes that masked his hunger.

'I'll move the bolster on the day you appoint another

personal assistant,' she said steadily, and he stiffened, outrage and desire fighting their own fierce battle.

'You can't expect me to fire a woman who I both like and respect, and who has proved herself to be an excellent employee, because of a whim. She was my brother's wife!' he snapped.

'And as your wife I expect you to put my wishes above those of a member of your staff.'

'It's hardly fair to make Robyn a scapegoat for the problems within our marriage.'

'Without Robyn, we wouldn't have any problem. It's her or me, Luc,' she warned. 'Your choice as to whether our marriage lives or dies. And until you've made a decision, this stays put.' She thumped the bolster emphatically and received a glare of such bitter fury that she withdrew to the furthest side of the bed and burrowed under the covers while he swore long and hard and she was grateful for once of her poor grasp of French.

Another week slipped past. Luc made no further reference to her demand that he dismiss Robyn but tension simmered between them. Gone was the laughter and friendship that had begun to develop between them and the ghost of Sabine continued to haunt her. If it hadn't been for Jean-Claude the atmosphere in the château would have been unbearable, Emily thought miserably. The weather, perhaps sympathising with her mood, had changed from glorious sunshine to long grey days of relentless rain and the château seemed dark and gloomy as winter approached. Luc's brooding presence in the nursery didn't help, although she noted that the only time he smiled these days was when he was playing with his son, and it reinforced her belief that he only tolerated her presence at the château for the sake of his son.

Perhaps he was frustrated, she thought bleakly, remembering his taunt about sexual frustration being hell. He possessed a huge sex drive. She could not forget those early months of their marriage, when his desire for her had been almost insatiable. Often he had made love to her for the whole night, leaving her exhausted while he then went off to put in a full twelve hours at the office. It was impossible to believe he had spent the year of their separation celibate, although it would certainly explain his foul mood, she acknowledged grimly. But she had problems of her own and suddenly Luc's sex life was the least of them.

Her period was only a few days late, she reassured herself as she noted the date on Luc's newspaper. Five days at most. There was no need to panic but she had quietly requested Liz to bring back a pregnancy test kit from the village.

'What is it?' Luc had lowered his paper fractionally and speared her with a hard stare as he took in her pale face. 'Has something in the news upset you?' he queried, flicking the front page round to scan the headlines. 'Your French must be improving, *chérie,* if you can follow an article about government fraud.'

'It's not that. It's nothing,' she muttered, trying to quell a feeling of nausea as Simone set a cup of rich, aromatic coffee in front of her. 'I'm not feeling all that well this morning. I've probably picked up a bug.'

'Hmm.' Luc looked plainly unconvinced and she shifted uncomfortably beneath his all-seeing gaze. Sometimes she felt he could read her mind and right now that would not be good. If, and it was a big if, she was pregnant, she didn't want to share the news until she'd had time to come to terms with it herself.

How could she have been so stupid? She castigated herself.

One accidental pregnancy was bad enough, but at least when she had fallen pregnant with Jean-Claude it hadn't been her fault. This time it was purely down to carelessness. She hadn't given contraception a thought, and although a small voice in her head argued that neither had Luc, he wasn't the one who would have to carry another child. It wasn't that she did not want another baby, she mused, a soft smile lighting her face as she watched Jean-Claude pour yoghurt over the tray of his highchair and then play in it. He was the best thing in her life and a little brother or sister could only increase her joy, but she doubted the same could be said of Luc. He had always maintained that he didn't want children, and despite his obvious adoration of his son, she shuddered to think of his reaction if she broke the news that he was to be a father for a second time.

'I have something I want to show you.' Luc's voice broke into her reverie and she blinked at him, wishing that the sight of him in jeans and a black polo shirt, open at the neck, did not play such havoc with her hormones. He had been away for the past two days. An urgent business meeting, Philippe had explained, but despite the tension that simmered between them whenever they were in the same room, she had missed him.

It was a pity the trip hadn't done anything to improve his mood, she mused, unaware that he had returned to London or that his conversation with his housekeeper at the penthouse was responsible for his brooding stares across the breakfast table. If it wasn't such a ridiculous idea, she could have sworn he was hiding behind his newspaper.

'It can wait until tomorrow if you're unwell,' he added, and she shook her head, willing to do anything to prolong the moment when he would retreat to his study for the rest of the day.

'I'm fine,' she replied brightly, surreptitiously pushing the coffee away from her. With her attention firmly set on mopping up Jean-Claude, she did not notice Luc's frown.

Luc took the steep steps leading to the west tower of the château two at a time, needing to find a release for his pent-up aggression. What the hell was he going to say to Emily? How could he admit that he had been wrong about her, that he had misjudged her and had done so on the word of the woman she had always suspected of trying to wreck their relationship?

He had trusted Robyn's word above Emily's, he acknowledged bitterly. True, he had begun to have serious doubts about Robyn's motives and now he had definitive proof that she had lied to him, but he was at a loss to know how he could repair the hurt he had caused.

He glanced back to find Emily struggling to keep up with him and his emotions crumbled at the sight of her flushed but determined face.

'Why have you brought me to the top of the tower?' she demanded as she joined Luc on the small landing and glanced out of the window at the incredible view of the Loire Valley spread below her. 'I hope you're not planning to push me off,' she quipped with a nervous laugh.

'Why do you think I would want do that, *chérie?*' The curiously husky tone in his voice brought her head up and she stared at him, noting for the first time the lines of strain around his eyes and the deep grooves that had appeared around his mouth. He would never be anything other than utterly gorgeous but he looked so tired and on edge that she longed to go to him. Instead, she shoved her hands behind her back, out of temptation's way.

'We haven't been getting on very well lately,' she offered quietly. 'I have a feeling that you're still angry with me.'

'I'm angry, *oui*,' he admitted harshly, 'but not with you, *ma petite*. My anger is directed solely at myself.'

Without giving her time to reply, he opened the door and ushered her into a large, circular room with windows all the way round so that light streamed in.

'What a spectacular view,' Emily murmured as she moved forward to admire the stunning scenery of the valley. 'What is this place, Luc?'

'It's your workroom—unless you would prefer rooms in another part of the château,' he added as silence stretched between them. 'I thought you would like it here. The view is, as you say, spectacular, and the light is good for you to work. Say something,' he demanded, his control slipping. He raked a hand nervously through his hair as he caught sight of her tears. 'Why are you *crying?* I thought you'd be pleased.'

'I am pleased. I'm...stunned,' she admitted thickly, scrubbing her eyes with the back of her hand. The betraying gesture made him want to drag her into his arms and plead for her forgiveness. It was too late for that, he conceded grimly as he swung round and shoved his hands in his pockets. There were things he had to do first, events he had to set in motion before he could even begin to beg for atonement, and kissing her senseless would not help his cause.

'I think you'll find everything you need here,' he told her, keeping his eyes firmly on the view rather than her face. 'Your sketches are there, along with the fabric samples you brought from Spain. The table should be big enough to use as a cutting table and, as you can see, your sewing-machine is on the bench under the window. I've arranged for two girls from the village to come and see you. They've both studied textiles and design and could possibly become your assistants, although the final decision lies with you, of course.'

Emily glanced around the room, her eyes filling once more. It was the unexpectedness of Luc's change of heart that had knocked her sideways and she didn't know what to think, what to say.

'I don't understand,' she murmured at last. 'You were so against the idea of me trying to start up my own business.'

'I realise now how selfish I was being,' he said slowly, as he swung round to her. 'This is important to you and, despite what you think, I want you to be happy at the château. I understand that Nadine Trouvier has invited you to visit her babywear shop in Paris and I'm prepared to allow you to go.'

Did that mean he finally trusted her? Emily wondered dazedly. Or did he assume she would leave Jean-Claude at the château and simply did not care whether or not she came back? 'It's all so much to take in,' she said shakily, sinking onto a stool before her legs gave way. 'You've gone to so much trouble, yet my idea may not even work. I might just be kidding myself that I'm any good and there's a chance that no one will want my designs.'

'Nadine would not have suggested marketing them in her shops unless she believed they would sell. Beneath her smile lurks a shrewd businesswoman.' He paused and then murmured, 'I think you should go to Paris with Jean-Claude. It will do you both good to spend a couple of days in the city.'

'But I thought you didn't trust me?' she faltered, her eyes wide with confusion as she stared at him. 'Aren't you worried I'll disappear with him?'

'*Non,*' he replied steadily, closing his mind to the fear that she would do exactly that. He hadn't offered her much incentive to want to stay with him but perhaps the workshop would go some way towards mending the wounds he had inflicted on their relationship. 'I don't believe you would deliberately try to hurt me and you would never do anything that would be detrimental to our son.'

'Well, you've certainly changed your tune.' The hint of bitterness in her tone faded as hope flooded her. 'Care to explain your sudden change of heart?'

'I hope to do so soon, *ma petite,*' he assured her, and the smoky quality in his voice caused her pulse rate to accelerate alarmingly. Luc trusted her enough to offer her her freedom and she felt as though a great weight had been lifted from her shoulders. Did that mean he finally believed her story about taking Jean-Claude to the penthouse? Suddenly it didn't seem to matter any more and she gave him a tremulous smile, her heart in her eyes.

'Maybe we could all go to Paris?' she suggested lightly. 'I have wonderful memories of the last time we were there.'

She walked over to him and ran her hand lightly over his chest. It was obvious that he had created the workroom for her as an olive branch and she was eager to accept it. He was prepared to view their marriage as a partnership and she was desperate to show that both he and Jean-Claude would always come first in her priorities, but even so her hand was visibly shaking as she laid it against his shirt.

'I'm sorry, *chérie,* but I have an urgent meeting in Orléans,' he murmured, and she quickly dropped her hand, her face flaming. 'Philippe will drive you to Paris.'

'Philippe? But I thought—' She broke off as the realisation hit that he did not trust her quite as much as she'd first believed. 'I can drive myself. I'm perfectly capable.'

'You're not used to driving in France, and you know how busy the roads are around Paris. You'll be safer with Philippe.'

'It's not my safety that bothers you, is it?' she demanded. 'Your only concern is for Jean-Claude.'

'It's natural for me to worry about him. Having just found him, I would give anything, including my life, to ensure his well-being,' he said, his voice unexpectedly fierce. She stared at him. 'Do you blame me for that?'

'Of course not.' Emily swallowed back the sudden tears that clogged her throat. Jean-Claude's safety was paramount to her, too, but Luc could not have sent out a clearer message that he was only interested in his son. Nothing had changed and although she certainly didn't resent the fact that Jean-Claude came first in his list of priorities, it hurt unbelievably to know that she came last. It was continuing the theme of her childhood, she thought miserably. She had always been made to feel she was a spare part. Was it so wrong to long to be loved totally and unequivocally for herself? She hung her head, desperate to hide her misery, but he cupped her chin and tilted her face to his.

'What is it, *ma petite?*' Don't you like the workroom?'

'It's wonderful,' she answered truthfully, 'but it doesn't change anything.' She could not live her life loving him so much that it was like a sickness inside her, while he treated her like a favourite cousin. It wasn't his fault that he did not love her, she accepted sadly, but for the sake of her own self-preservation, she couldn't stay with him.

'It's not going to work,' she told him bluntly, and his eyes narrowed.

'The workshop, you mean?'

'I mean us, you and me. I can't stay with you, knowing that you don't trust me.'

'It's not a question of trust,' he said heavily, and she sighed her frustration.

'It's a question of emotions, or rather your lack of them.'

'I love Jean-Claude,' he shouted furiously. 'How can you doubt it?'

'I don't,' she said, her anger draining as swiftly as it had come. She felt like she was hitting her head against a brick wall and she was too bruised to care any more.

'I won't allow you to throw away what we have. I give you my word that our marriage has my full commitment.'

'As long as I stay at the château and only take Jean-Claude out escorted by a glorified jailer, while we remain as distant as ever, only coming together for occasional sex,' she muttered. 'It doesn't sound like much of a life, Luc.'

'The only life you'll have,' he ground out. 'I won't let you go, Emily.' He followed her across the room as she sought to put some space between them, closing in so that her spine came up against the long table that ran the length of the room. 'If sex is the only way I can bind you to me then so be it. I never asked if you're on the Pill and in the heat of the moment I didn't use any contraception when we made love. You could be pregnant,' he told her huskily. 'Have you thought of that?'

She had thought of nothing else for the past few days but now was not the time to admit her suspicions. Luc was too close, too overpowering and she gasped as he suddenly lifted her onto the table, his hands clamping like a vice around her hips.

'You don't want more children,' she said nervously, her tongue darting out to moisten her dry lips. His eyes narrowed as they homed in on her mouth. 'You didn't want the first one.'

'I always wanted him, and if I hadn't wanted more I would

have taken more care to ensure you didn't conceive,' he told her coolly. 'I would like nothing better than to see you swollen with our child.'

His hand moved to her flat stomach and she could not repress the quiver of awareness that ran through her. This close she could detect the exotic musk of his aftershave mingled with another, more subtle male scent that was essentially his. His hand had moved from her stomach to the swell of her breast and as he cupped the soft mound she felt her nipples harden until they were straining against her thin T-shirt, begging for his touch. He captured her mouth in a fierce assault, hot and passionate, demanding her response, and she gave a moan of despair as her lips parted, allowing his tongue to delve between them in a fierce exploration that left her trembling.

'Please, Luc,' she begged. She couldn't allow him to dominate her like this. One touch was all it took to set her on fire and she twisted restlessly as he pushed her legs apart and stood between them. His hand slid beneath her skirt and she held her breath as he dipped beneath and discovered the shaming evidence that she was desperate for him. His low growl of triumph was too much to bear and the tears poured down Emily's cheeks while her lips still clung to his as she kissed him with all the pent-up emotions inside her.

'Please, don't do this,' she whispered brokenly, and he stiffened, his eyes glazed and heavy-lidded as he stared at her.

'Because you don't want me?' he challenged furiously. 'Because you want your freedom? You are my wife, *chérie*. For all our sakes I suggest you accept that fact.' He jerked away from her and strode towards the door while she tried to bring her body under control. It was all she could do not to call him back but she swallowed the words.

'Where are you going?' she cried instead, and shrank from the anger in his gaze.

'To hell! That's where you'd like to send me, isn't it?' came the terse reply before he disappeared. And as she heard his feet on the stairs she buried her face in her hands and wept.

CHAPTER NINE

EMILY SPENT THE REST OF THE DAY nursing Jean-Claude, who was cutting a tooth and determined that everyone should know about it. Luc had disappeared and her mood see-sawed from misery to anger and finally to a faint tenuous hope that there was still a chance for their marriage. She had overreacted earlier, she berated herself. She had behaved like the silly, immature child Luc had once called her, but hopefully he would listen to her apology.

That hope swiftly died when she entered the dining room for dinner and noted that only one place had been set at the long, mahogany table.

'Will Monsieur Vaillon be joining me?' she asked Philippe.

'I regret not, Madame. He has gone to Orléans and does not expect to return until tomorrow.'

'I see.' He had left already and her dismay was clearly evident in the huskiness of her voice. 'In that case I think I'll have my dinner on a tray in the television room,' she murmured. 'I'll just go and change. I'm rather over-dressed,' she added with a vain attempt at humour.

The butler's usually impassive expression lightened into something akin to a smile of sympathy, which only made her feel worse, and she fled upstairs, wondering for the hundredth time why she had decided to wear the blue silk evening dress Luc had chosen for her. She had wanted to please him, she acknowledged as she hung it back in the wardrobe and pulled on her jeans. She'd wanted to thank him for listening to her ideas about the babywear company she hoped to establish and which initially he had been so much against. He had vowed that he wanted to give their marriage another chance and creating the workshop for her was proof of his commitment, but once again they had been driven apart by misunderstanding and her wretched insecurity.

Philippe wheeled the serving trolley into the television room. Sylvie had prepared her favourite *bouillabaisse,* he announced, but as she lifted the lid of the dish nausea gripped her and she fled from the room. This was no ordinary stomach upset, she thought grimly some ten minutes later when she had staggered from the bathroom to lie limply on the bed. The sickness had passed, probably because she had nothing left in her stomach, but she felt weak and tearful and her breasts ached.

There was only one way to put her mind at rest, she decided, jumping up from the bed and returning to the bathroom to retrieve the pregnancy test kit from where she had hidden it at the back of the cupboard. She had to know if she was carrying another child. Five minutes had never passed so slowly but even so, she was unprepared for the shocking truth.

A baby! Luc's second child! She didn't know whether to laugh or cry and managed both as her emotions swung from joy to despair. What would he say? Would he be pleased or angry? Would he accuse her of falling pregnant on purpose, as he had when she she'd conceived Jean-Claude, and would he withdraw from her as he had done the first time?

She had to know. She could not wait patiently until he returned from Orléans to tell him her news and gauge his reaction. It was still early in the evening and ignoring the small voice of caution she ran down to his study. It was ridiculous for her heart to beat so fast, she thought irritably, to feel that she was intruding in his inner sanctum. She flicked on the light. Her attention was immediately caught by the array of photographs on his desk and tears burned her eyes as she studied them. They were not of Jean-Claude, as she had assumed, but of her. One showed her in the stables at Heston Grange, her hair all over the place and a shy smile on her face as she posed awkwardly for the camera. The others were from the magical weekend they had shared in Paris at the start of their marriage, and she was stunned by the emotion evident in her eyes. She brimmed with love, glowed with it, and she was shaken to see how badly she had failed to hide her feelings for him. Had he kept the pictures to gloat over her weakness? she wondered. Or was there another reason why he surrounded himself with her image?

As she replaced the framed photos on his desk she noted a name scrawled across his notepad. La Fayette had to be the name of a hotel, she surmised, praying that the receptionist would be able to speak English as she dialled the number.

'*Oui*. Monsieur Vaillon is booked into the Plaza suite,' the receptionist confirmed, 'but he is in a meeting and left strict instructions that he does not wish to be disturbed.'

'I'm his wife,' Emily swiftly explained. 'He'll talk to me.'

'Monsieur was very precise,' the receptionist murmured doubtfully, and Emily's temper frayed along with her nerves.

'It's an emergency. I insist you put me through.'

There followed several minutes of silence that played havoc with her stomach before there was a click and Luc's terse voice sounded down the line.

'Emily, what's wrong? The receptionist said it was an emergency. Is it Jean-Claude? Is he ill?' There was no disguising the fear in his voice and she hastened to reassure him.

'Jean-Claude's fine. I just wanted to talk to you…' She came to a halt as his impatient sigh growled in her ear.

'I'm busy, *chérie*. Can't it wait?'

'Yes, it can wait,' she whispered slowly, her excitement draining away as reality kicked her in the teeth once again. 'I'm sorry. I shouldn't have bothered you.'

'I'll be home tomorrow,' he said more gently, as if sensing her distress. 'We'll talk then, I promise.'

'Fine.' She cut the call and sat staring at the photos of herself. What a stupid, deluded fool she had been, she thought bitterly. All she had ever hoped for had been a little of his love, but it seemed it was too much to ask.

The stairs were as steep as a mountain and Emily's legs felt like lead. Sabine's perfect features seemed to mock her as she passed by the portrait of Luc's first wife, but when she reached the bedroom the sight of the vast bed and the bolster that divided it was the last straw and she curled up into a ball and sobbed. She was trapped in a loveless marriage, bound by the ties of her son and the new fragile life within her, and right now she felt miserable, afraid and desperately alone.

'Why don't you let me take care of Jean-Claude for a couple of hours?' Liz asked next morning, her friendly face creased in concern as she watched Emily struggle to force down her breakfast. 'He'll be quite happy with me,' she added, and Emily's heart lurched.

How could she even contemplate taking Jean-Claude away from the château? This was his home and he loved it here, she acknowledged, watching the way he was giggling with

Simone. Every member of Luc's staff adored him and it wouldn't be fair to uproot him yet again. She was caught in the middle, unable to leave him and unwilling to go without him, but how could she remain in her soulless marriage?

The rain had cleared to leave grey clouds scudding across the sky and for once she was glad to leave Jean-Claude in Liz's charge while she took refuge in the place she loved best—the stables.

'I hate him,' she told Kasim fiercely, anger her only defence against the ever-present tears that threatened to spill. She refused to cry over Luc any more and a sudden impulse saw her tack up the horse and lead him outside.

'Wait! Madame, it's not safe to go out alone.' As she crossed the yard the groom sped after her and she glanced down at his anxious face impatiently. What he meant was that Luc had forbidden her to take Kasim out alone, but she was tired of following orders and Luc wasn't there.

'It's all right. I won't be long,' she shouted as she reached the field and urged the horse into a canter. 'Stop worrying. I can handle Kasim.'

An hour later Luc strode into the stables, his thunderous expression giving some indication of his mood. 'What do you mean, she's gone?' Fresh from the worst night of his life, his temper exploded with the force of a pyroclastic flow and he had to restrain himself from grabbing the groom by his neck and shaking the information out of him. 'I gave strict instructions that Madame Vaillon should not take her horse out alone.'

'I tried to tell her, but Madame, she just went.' The groom shrugged his shoulders expressively and for a second Luc felt a twinge of sympathy for him. He did not underestimate

Emily's determination to get her own way and apprehension gripped him as the first spots of rain began to fall. 'You should have gone after her,' he muttered as he mounted his horse. 'Which way did she go?'

'Monsieur!' Something in the groom's voice made him glance back and apprehension turned to full-blown fear as Kasim galloped, riderless, into the yard. The rain was falling harder, driving into his face, and with a savage oath Luc kicked his horse into a gallop and headed across the field as if the hounds of hell were pursuing him.

After spending days cooped up because of the rain, Kasim was even more high-spirited than usual and it took all Emily's strength to hold him back. The ground was waterlogged and several times she felt his feet slip, but that only seemed to increase his frustration. Of all the stupid things she had done in her life, this was the worst, she thought as common sense returned and she carefully dismounted. How could she have put the tiny scrap of humanity she was carrying inside her at risk, even for one second? Whatever Luc's reaction, she would love this baby with every fibre of her being.

Kasim was snorting and tossing his head and the sound of a motorbike hurtling along the lane increased his panic so that he reared up and the reins were snatched from Emily's hands.

'Kasim, whoa, boy,' she called frantically, but he was already halfway across the field. As she stumbled after him she tripped and fell into a pile of brambles. Crying wasn't an option right now, she decided as she gingerly pulled herself to her feet. The rain had increased and Kasim had disappeared into the mist. She could only pray he would head back along familiar paths to the stables, but ahead of her lay a long walk across muddy fields on an ankle that hurt like hell when she put weight on it.

It was a good thing Luc was away, she thought dismally when she peered through the rain to find that the edge of the field seemed no nearer. He would be furious with her for disobeying his orders. Maybe he would even sell Kasim, as he had once threatened. The thought spurred her to hobble faster but as she approached the gate a figure appeared out of the mist and her steps slowed.

From a distance he looked as though he had stepped from one of the tapestries that adorned the walls of the château— a medieval knight whose incredible facial bone structure hinted at a family ancestry that had links with ancient kings. As he urged his horse forward, she could see that instead of chain mail it was his thick black sweater that glinted with sparkling beads of rain. His hair was slicked back from his face to reveal the hard planes of his face. It was unfair that despite being soaked to the skin, he still looked devastatingly sexy, and she was painfully aware of her mud-spattered clothes and hair that fell round her shoulders in rats' tails.

'What the *hell* are you playing at?' he growled when she stopped a safe distance from him. It was sheer bravado that made her fold her arms across her chest and glare up at him.

'I could ask you the same thing. How was your meeting? It must have been vitally important to keep you from speaking to your wife. But perhaps not,' she added bleakly. 'I come a long way down your list of priorities, don't I, Luc?'

'Don't be ridiculous. Of course you're important to me. Were you hurt when you came off Kasim?'

'He didn't throw me,' she muttered hastily, her spurt of bravery trickling away beneath the glowering fury of his frown.

'Then what happened? Kasim turned up at the stables over half an hour ago. Are you telling me you chose to walk back through the rain with a sprained ankle for the sheer fun of it?'

'It's not sprained. I just tripped and landed heavily on it. Is Kasim all right? You won't sell him, will you?' she pleaded, her eyes enormous in her pale face. He muttered a profanity under his breath.

'The horse is fine, although I've yet to decide whether I'll keep him. I knew he was too strong for you.'

'He isn't—'

'Shut up and give me your hand.' He cut her off, his grey eyes glinting like molten steel, and Emily felt her own temper rise. Last night he hadn't been able to fit her into his busy schedule and the concern on his face probably had more to do with the fact that she had placed an expensive horse in danger.

'I can manage, thanks.'

'*Em-il-y!* I could kill you, if you weren't so intent on doing it yourself.' He leaned over, gripped her arm and hauled her into the saddle in front of him as easily as if she were a doll. Instantly his arms came round her, clamping her against the wall of his chest so that she could hear his heart thudding beneath her ear. He smelled of the rain, earthy and sensual, and she closed her eyes despairingly as her senses leapt, awareness flooding through her so that tried to hold herself rigid and not give in to the temptation to turn her face into his neck.

He flicked the reins and they walked on, the pace slow and steady through the rain, but all Emily could think of was the hardness of Luc's thighs pressing on hers as she sat between his legs. The motion of the horse meant that his body pushed against hers in a rhythm that grew ever more erotic and her breathing quickened. Emily tried to calm her wayward thoughts. Luc had made it clear that he only wanted her on his terms, when it suited him, but right now he was fiercely aroused and instead of disgust she was overwhelmed by another, far more elemental emotion, her instincts warning that his hunger for her was close to breaking point. Heat radiated from where his hand lay heavy on her waist and every nerve ending prickled unbearably when it slid lower and came to rest between her legs.

'Take your hands off me. You can't pick me up when the mood takes you and you're not too busy. Last night you couldn't even be bothered to talk to me,' she accused, aiming for anger. Instead, her voice sounded broken and full of misery.

'I spent most of last night driving around Orléans trying to pluck up the courage to face you.' His soft, seductive accent trickled over her skin, his breath fanning her neck so that she shivered, her senses heightened to an unbearable degree.

'I don't believe you and as soon as we get back to the château I'm leaving you. I refuse to be…*humiliated* by you any longer.'

'I won't let you go, *chérie.*' The implacability of his tone made her shiver and she fell silent as they entered the stable-yard and he dismounted before lifting her down. Instantly she swung on her heel, intent on marching back to the château. 'Wait! I want to talk to you.' His voice flayed her like a whip and she swung round, indignation bristling from every pore. But he ignored her while he spoke to the groom.

She would not sit panting at his heels like a faithful dog, she thought furiously. He still had his back to her and she slipped into the barn. He might want to talk to her but she wasn't in the mood to listen. She was still puzzled by his admission that he had needed to pluck up his courage before he returned to the château. Perhaps he was going to announce that he wanted a divorce after all, and she was suddenly glad that she hadn't told him she was pregnant. It was her secret and she was determined to withhold it until she knew where their relationship was heading.

The minutes ticked by and she lay back in the loose hay, wondering if it was safe to emerge from her hiding place yet. He must have started walking back to the château, believing that she was in front of him, but her heart sank as the barn door creaked open. Damn it! He couldn't find her here. She huddled deeper into the hay and squeezed her eyes shut in an effort to stifle a sneeze, but it was no good and the sound of his mocking laughter grated on her already raw nerves.

'I couldn't have chosen a better place for a private conversation, *chérie*,' he murmured as he rounded the hay bale and stood in front of it, barring her escape, 'I want to talk to you about Robyn.'

'Then prepare yourself for the shortest conversation on record because of all the subjects I'd like to talk about, Robyn isn't one of them.'

His smile did strange things to her insides and she dragged her eyes from the way his wet jeans clung lovingly to his thighs. Suddenly her teeth were chattering—reaction to everything that had happened in the last twenty-four hours, she told herself, and the fact that she was sitting in wet clothes. It had nothing to do with Luc's close proximity or the way his eyes were skimming her wet shirt, tracing the outline of her breasts with barely concealed hunger. 'Why do you suppose I would want to talk about her?' she flung at him, and to her consternation he stretched full length beside her, propped up on his side so that he could lean over her to stroke her cheek with a wisp of hay.

'I know that she lied,' he offered quietly, pausing for a heartbeat to assess her reaction before he continued. 'I know you came back the Chelsea penthouse with Jean-Claude soon after he was born. I met her last night in Orléans. She was the reason I couldn't talk to you.'

'My God, you bastard!' Emily gasped as she forced air into her lungs. 'You spent the night with her. And to think I actually believed you when you denied having an affair with her. Will I ever learn?' she whispered despairingly. 'And will you ever stop breaking my heart?' She made to roll away from him but he gripped her arm.

'I did not spend the night with her. I asked her to meet me at the hotel because I couldn't bear to have her at the château,' he explained, the nerve jumping in his cheek giving some indication of his tension. 'After you told me about your visit to the penthouse I decided to check a few things with my house-keeper.'

'Mrs Patterson wasn't there,' Emily pointed out quickly.

'I know, but she told me she had been puzzled because she was sure someone had stayed in the flat while I was in South Africa. It confirmed your story,' he said quietly.

He was watching her, waiting for her to speak, but Emily felt curiously numb. 'So,' she muttered, 'you finally believe that I brought Jean-Claude to you. Robyn lied, but where does that leave us? I can't see happy ever after flashing up in bright lights.' She blinked fiercely, determined not to cry in front of him, and he sighed.

'Robyn lied to both of us, *ma petite,* but if it's any consolation, she's bitterly sorry for the harm she caused.'

'She's in love with you,' Emily said quietly, wondering how he could have been so blind to the signs. She closed her eyes and tried to imagine how different things might have turned out if Luc had been at the flat that day rather than Robyn. Despite his coolness towards her during her pregnancy, she no longer doubted that he wanted his son. He loved Jean-Claude, but she still didn't understand his relationship with Robyn any more than she understood where she featured in his life.

She loved him but he didn't love her. Nothing had changed and she couldn't go on living a lie, pretending to be content when she was falling apart. 'I think I'd like to go back to England for a while, take Jean-Claude to see my family. I'm not taking him away from you but…' She hesitated fractionally. 'I think we need to spend some time apart.'

'You're leaving me!' Luc said heavily, a nerve jumping in his cheek. 'I don't deserve anything less but you have to believe that I am desperately sorry for believing Robyn over you and I swear, *chérie,* I'll do anything to make it up to you.'

The urgency in his voice startled her but, of course, she reminded herself, he was afraid that if she took Jean-Claude to England, she would never bring him back.

'It's not just Robyn,' she said miserably. 'I accept that you never slept with her and I understand how easily she fooled both of us, but that's the point, isn't it? If we had trusted each other more, we would have uncovered her lies before any real harm had been done. I need some time to think,' she admitted slowly, but as she moved to stand up, he pulled her down into the hay and trapped her beneath him.

'I can't let you go,' he muttered hoarsely. 'You belong here at the château, you and Jean-Claude.'

The subtle change in his tone was enough to alert her defences and she pushed ineffectively against his shoulders, suddenly desperate to escape him before she did something stupid, like beg him to make love to her.

'You were mine, Emily, from the moment you first gave yourself to me, and I guard my possessions jealously. Maybe it's time I demonstrated that fact.'

His low taunt fuelled her defiance and she would have twisted her head, but he reacted faster, his mouth finding hers with unerring precision. His kiss stole the breath from her body and took with it the last remnants of her pride as he proved beyond doubt that he was her master. She wanted him with an urgency that was all the more shocking because she no longer cared that he didn't love her. All she cared about was assuaging this driving need to feel him deep inside her and desire rendered them equal. This had been building from the moment he had dragged her onto his horse. It would be the last time she would ever make love with him, a final goodbye. He would never want her once he knew she was pregnant and she couldn't stay and allow his indifference to tear her apart again.

When he eventually lifted his head her mouth was swollen and he stared down at her, his eyes glittering, warning her that this time there would be no reprieve.

'You said you wanted to talk,' she reminded him thickly, and he gave a harsh laugh as he dragged his sweater over his head before coming down on her once more.

'We've tried talking and it gets us nowhere. This is the only lasting truth between us, *chérie,* the only form of communication where we don't argue. You want me as much as I want you,' he whispered, his breath warm on her skin as he unbuttoned her shirt and tugged the fabric apart. She shivered, unable to deny the truth.

He dispensed with her bra with a deftness that warned of his determination and cupped her breasts in his hands, moulding them before bending to lather first one nipple and then the other with his tongue.

'Luc.' She groaned his name and slid her hand behind his head to hold him to his task, but he moved lower to drag her sodden jeans over her thighs with a force that should have frightened her. Her underwear went the same way and she gasped as he shoved her legs apart, exposing her to his gaze as he knelt over her.

'No!' Her whimper of denial fell on deaf ears and if she was honest she didn't want him to stop. His tongue was a wicked instrument of torture and he used it mercilessly, exploring her with intimate precision until she was writhing and trembling, her body poised on the edge of ecstasy. Frantically she tugged his hair, needing him to stop, now, before it was too late. But his lips closed around the ultra-sensitive nub of her clitoris and sensation pierced her as he suckled.

'Oh, God! Now, Luc, please.' She couldn't take much more, could already feel the first spasms of pleasure tighten her muscles.

He stood up, shrugged out of his jeans and stared at her for timeless seconds. She must look like some wild, wanton creature, she thought despairingly, but it didn't matter when he knelt in front of her, slid his hands beneath her bottom and lifted her hips so that he could enter her with one powerful thrust. Instantly she wrapped her legs around his waist to draw him deeper and he eased back a fraction before pushing again and again, setting a rhythm that she eagerly matched.

She had been so ready for him that it was impossible to control her reactions and she peaked instantly, her body overwhelmed by wave after wave of pleasure. Gasping, she clutched his shoulders as he rode her, each thrust driving her higher still, and incredibly, as her climax subsided she felt another build. It was impossible surely to experience such a glorious, mind-blowing sensation again and she stared into his face, noting the rigid line of his jaw as he fought for control. He lost it spectacularly at the same time as she came again and she felt him shudder as her muscles closed round him, her name emitted as a low groan when he finally slumped on top of her.

For a short while there was nothing but the warmth of his body covering hers, the sound of their breathing gradually slowing and the sweet scent of the hay that cocooned them in their own private nirvana. Eventually he stirred and she paled at the bleakness in his eyes as he rolled off her. His expression shouted louder than words that he regretted giving in to the primitive need that had gripped them both, and she shivered and reached for her shirt. It was damp and cold on her heated skin but she dragged it across her breasts, wanting to punish her body for its bitter betrayal.

'You don't really want to leave me, any more that I could stand to see you go,' he said flatly, his eyes never leaving her face. 'Look into your heart, *chérie*. It recognised the truth between us.'

She knew exactly what was in her heart, Emily thought bleakly. It was Luc's that was the mystery. She sighed and swung away from him to pull on her jeans.

'*Sacré bleu!* What have you done to your back? You're bleeding.' His face was white with anguish.

She glanced over her shoulder, alerted by the horror in his voice, and saw that her shirt was streaked with blood. 'I'm fine. It's nothing, just some scratches from when I fell into some bushes,' she reassured him, but he pulled her against his chest and ran his hands over her as if desperate to assure himself that she was unhurt.

'You're so pale, and I'm no better than my barbaric ancestor,' he growled, his voice laced with self-disgust. She was so tiny, so fragile, and he had let her down so badly, it was no wonder she was staring up at him with huge, fearful eyes. 'Here, drink this,' he ordered, dragging a hip flask from his pocket. Her face turned a sickly shade of green as he unscrewed the lid and she caught the unmistakable smell of brandy.

'That's not a good idea,' she murmured faintly, and he clamped down on his impatience as he held the flask against her lips. She looked like death and fear gripped him.

'What's the matter with you?' he shouted as her legs buckled. Had she lied? Had Kasim thrown her and she had kept quiet for fear of his anger? '*Mon Dieu!* Emily, you must drink this.'

'No.' She clamped her blue lips resolutely together as her head lolled forward. 'No alcohol, Luc...I'm pregnant!'

CHAPTER TEN

'WHY THE *HELL* didn't you tell me?'

Emily opened her eyes to discover she was in her bedroom at the château. Luc was leaning over her, his face contorted with fury, and she lowered her lashes again, wishing she could return to oblivion.

'Monsieur Vaillon, the doctor is here.' Liz's calm tones cut through the simmering tension and she heard him mutter something in his own language before he stepped back from the bed.

'Call me the minute he's finished,' Luc instructed Liz, and it was only when she heard the door creak on its hinges that Emily dared to open her eyes again.

'He's just upset,' Liz reassured her quickly, noting the stark misery on her face. 'You gave him a terrible fright when you collapsed in the stables. He literally ran all the way back to the château with you in his arms.'

'He's angry with me,' Emily whispered, her eyes filling with tears that spilled down her cheeks. Liz patted her arm.

'Shock does funny things to people and you have to admit it was quite a dramatic way of announcing your pregnancy. He was scared, that's all. He's very protective of you.'

Luc hadn't looked protective, Emily thought bleakly when the doctor had finished his examination and assured her she was a perfectly healthy woman in the first stages of pregnancy. Luc had looked as though he wanted to commit murder.

'How did Luc seem?' she asked hesitantly when Liz returned to the bedroom. 'I'm not sure how he'll feel about being a father again.'

'If you ask me, he'll be over the moon,' Liz replied softly. 'He adores Jean-Claude.'

'Yes, he does.' There was no dispute over Luc's feelings for his son, she acknowledged bleakly as she stared up at the canopy above the bed. But his feelings for his wife were a different matter. He would never let her go now, but he wanted her for all the wrong reasons.

The doctor had advised her to rest but inactivity gave her time to think, so she padded into the *en suite,* filled the bath and added a generous handful of scented crystals that promised to soothe and de-stress. She needed all the help she could get in that department, she conceded, and closed her eyes as the foam worked its magic.

'So, not content with terrifying me this afternoon, you're now trying to drown yourself.' The furious rumble from the doorway caused her eyes to fly open and she jerked upright, horrified to realise that the water had been lapping around her chin. Most of the bubbles had disappeared and she flung her arms across her chest, her cheeks flaming with the acknowledgement that it was way too late for modesty.

'What do you want?' she snapped, and Luc felt the familiar tug in his chest as her hands slid to her stomach in an instinctively protective gesture. *You* was the simple answer, but she was bristling like an angry porcupine and now didn't seem a good time to reveal what was in his heart, even supposing she would listen, he thought bleakly.

'To talk,' he murmured instead as he leaned away from the door and strolled towards her.

His damp hair indicated that had recently showered. His crisp white shirt was open at the throat and his black trousers moulded his thighs leaving little to her imagination that was determined to recall every second of the moments in the stable.

'It wasn't terribly productive last time we tried it,' Emily said pointedly, turning hot and cold at the memory of their *talk* in the hay barn.

'On the contrary, *chérie,* I found it most revealing, although you withheld one vital secret from me.'

She could say nothing in her defence and sat silently in the rapidly cooling water, defying him to come any closer, which of course he did, holding out a fluffy bath sheet.

'I can manage,' she began, her voice trailing off beneath the ferocity of his glare.

'Humour me, *ma petite.*' He patently wasn't going to move and with an exasperated sigh she stood and stepped over the side of the bath, allowing him to envelop her in the folds of the towel. Having him rub her dry with brisk efficiency was taking it a step too far, she decided when her body was tingling all over, but the blandness of his expression warned her he was determined to play nursemaid and she rewarded him with a dignified silence.

Once satisfied that she was dry, he slipped her nightdress over her head and she raised her brows in silent query at the exquisite creation of ivory silk.

'For the sake of my sanity I need you to be covered while we talk, but I couldn't find the unflattering T-shirt you insist on wearing—although I admit I didn't look very hard,' he added beneath his breath.

Before she could formulate a reply he swept her into his arms and carried her through to the bedroom where he deposited her between the sheets and adjusted her pillows. He treated her with something akin to reverence, as if she was infinitely precious to him, but it had to be an illusion, Emily thought as tears welled in her eyes. He didn't care about her, he only cared for Jean-Claude and she couldn't begin to hazard a guess at his thoughts about the new baby.

'Are you angry?' she queried tremulously when his silent scrutiny had stretched her nerves to breaking point.

'Move from that bed and you'll discover the true heat of my temper.' He stared at her downcast face and sighed. 'I'm not angry with you. I blame myself.'

'Good. I blame you too.' It was obvious from the way he was skirting around the issue that he wasn't happy about the baby and she was surprised at how much it hurt. She should have expected it when his reaction to Jean-Claude's conception was so clear in her mind. There was no hope for them now, she thought, and wished he would go so that she could cry alone.

'Don't you want this baby?' he asked, his voice laced with a curious huskiness that she could almost believe was pain.

She glanced at him, noting the deep grooves around his mouth. 'Of course I want him…or her. My views on parenthood have never been in doubt. But what about you, Luc?' she whispered. 'For a man who vowed he didn't want children, it must be a blow to learn you're going to be a father for the second time.'

'It's not that I didn't want children,' he said hoarsely as he jumped to his feet and paced restlessly next to the bed. His air of urbane calm had always been impressive but he seemed to have undergone a dramatic transformation. His body was as tense as whipcord, his jaw rigid, but it was the agony in his eyes that trapped her gaze. She stared at him, desperate to understand. 'I always wanted Jean-Claude, you have to believe me,' he muttered, his accent so pronounced that she had to concentrate on his words. 'But I was so afraid, *mon coeur,* so afraid for you.

'Last time, when the contraception failed there was some excuse, but this time it was sheer carelessness on my part,' he admitted, his voice thick with self-disgust. 'I made love to you because I couldn't help myself. You are in my blood, Emily, in my heart. One look at you and I knew I had to have you again. It's like an obsession, this need to hold you in my arms and experience the ecstasy only you can give. The last thing on my mind when I made love to you was the possible outcome yet I, more than anyone, should be aware of the consequences of such negligence. It is because of me that Sabine died,' he groaned, his face twisting. 'It was my fault.'

'No.' Emily couldn't bear the torment in his eyes any longer and she reached out to him, pulling him onto the bed. 'Luc, Sabine's death was a terrible tragedy but it was nobody's fault. An ectopic pregnancy is a comparatively rare condition. You couldn't have known it would happen and there was nothing you could have done to prevent it.'

'But that's not true, don't you see?' He broke off and ran a hand over his face, his fingers shaking with the force of his emotions. 'I didn't love her. I doubt I ever did. When we met I was young and arrogant and for me it was lust at first sight, but the cracks started to appear early in our marriage. Sabine was obsessed with having a child while I was more focused on my career. There were endless rows, she had other lovers and our marriage was all but dead. The holiday was a last-ditch attempt by Sabine to save it.' He fell silent, his expression unfathomable, and Emily shivered as she recalled the rest of the story Robyn had told her.

'But Sabine was pregnant,' she murmured tentatively, and he nodded.

'Yes, but I doubt the child was mine, which was possibly why she said nothing. When she collapsed I had no idea what was wrong. We were miles from medical assistance and there was nothing I could do. It was over so quickly,' he said rawly, 'and I felt so helpless. Later a post-mortem revealed that Sabine had already suffered one ectopic pregnancy, hence her difficulty in conceiving. I didn't even know she was pregnant and she never told me of the increased risk of another ectopic. It seemed unbelievable that a woman could die as a result of pregnancy in the twenty-first century and I felt so guilty. I vowed I would never put another woman at such risk.'

'Oh, God!' Understanding dawned and Emily closed her eyes as his words hit her. 'That was why you were so adamant that you didn't want children, wasn't it? But by the time it became an issue between us, I was already pregnant with Jean-Claude.'

'It seemed cruelly ironic that Sabine had been unable to conceive despite all her efforts and yet you fell so easily.'

'You seemed so angry and I was so hurt. I needed you,' she whispered, 'but I was sure you didn't want me or the baby and I had no idea what I had done wrong.'

'Forgive me, *ma petite*,' he groaned, and her heart turned over at the pain in his eyes. 'I knew you were unhappy living in London. There were issues with my company that meant I was busier than usual—and issues with Robyn that have only become clear since,' he added bitterly. 'A holiday, a belated honeymoon on a paradise island where we could be alone, seemed like a good idea.' He broke off with a harsh laugh. 'You'd think I would have learned from my experience of remote islands, but I hadn't anticipated history repeating itself quite so dramatically. When you collapsed with the heat, after whispering that you suspected you were pregnant, I...' He shook his head at the agonising memory. 'I thought I would lose you in the same terrible circumstances as Sabine. I was terrified, *chérie,* and in my fear I went a little mad, but I wasn't angry with you. I blamed myself for risking the life of the woman who meant more to me than anyone ever had.'

Did he mean her? Emily felt her heart lurch painfully in her chest and quickly quashed the little flicker of hope. The ghosts in his past she could deal with, especially now she understood that his coolness towards her during her pregnancy had been the result of fear for her safety, not revulsion for the changes in her body. But there were still things she did not understand. 'I wish you had confided in me,' she said sadly. 'It would have explained so much, saved so much misery. Instead, you turned to Robyn and shut me out. I couldn't understand your closeness to her and as we grew further and further apart it seemed likely that she was your mistress.'

'You must know now that we were never lovers,' he began urgently, and she nodded.

'I believe you, but adultery isn't necessarily a physical act,' she whispered. 'I used to watch the two of you together, Luc. I recognised the bond that existed between you and I felt rejected.'

He was quiet for so long that she thought he must have forgotten her, but as she tried to pull her hand free he tightened his grip and she was shocked by the bleakness of his expression.

'I swore I would never talk about my childhood. It was not the happiest of times,' he admitted grimly, 'but I don't want you to think I'm shutting you out ever again. My father was a cold, distant man. I don't ever remember an occasion when I saw him smile, or felt that I had earned his approval. My mother was quiet, sensitive and for the most part deeply unhappy. I've always thought that I must have failed her in some way,' he admitted quietly, and her heart turned over at the emotion in his voice. 'Perhaps she just didn't care for me enough to want to carry on with her life.'

'Luc, severe depression is an illness,' Emily said huskily, holding his hand between both of hers as she sought to comfort him. 'Maybe in her confused state she thought you would be better off without her, but I'm sure she loved you.' Beneath the urbane, successful businessman she recognised the lonely boy within and she ached for him.

'Perhaps,' he murmured with a shrug, 'but at least I had Yves. We were extraordinarily close, especially after my mother's death. As we grew older our friendship continued. We shared everything and I was delighted when he fell in love with Robyn. It seemed that at least one Vaillon marriage would prove successful. Yves's death was a shattering blow,' he confided, his eyes shadowed with remembered pain. 'Robyn clung to me for support and I suppose I confided in her in place of my brother, but I regarded her as a close friend, nothing more.' He stared at Emily intently, as if he was desperate for her to believe him.

'My seeming reluctance to become a father was not because I did not want our child but because I was afraid I would not be a good parent. I didn't have the best role models,' he said heavily, and she squeezed his fingers reassuringly.

'You're a wonderful father. Jean-Claude adores you, as will the new baby.'

'I feared that my upbringing had left me unable to love and my marriage to Sabine only seemed to prove it. I had lost Yves, the only person I truly cared for, and I decided that life was less complicated if my emotions were uninvolved. But now I realise how much I was fooling myself,' he told her, his voice softening as he took in her delicate features and wide, expressive eyes.

'You discovered that you love your son,' she murmured, and her heart leapt painfully in her chest at the expression in his eyes. He was trying to tell her something and she wished she could decipher the code.

'I met you,' he said gruffly, and the tension between them became unbearable. Abruptly he jumped to his feet, his movements clumsy and uncoordinated, and the tight band around her heart suddenly snapped. This was Luc, the man she loved more than life itself, and he was in agony. 'I felt sorry for Robyn and I trusted her as a friend but I never felt anything more for her,' he muttered. 'I hoped that as time passed she would come to terms with Yves's death and her dependency on me would lessen, but I missed the signs that she wanted more from our relationship. I don't know what I can do to repair the damage I've caused, the hurt I've inflicted on you,' he said huskily, 'but even though you must hate me, I can't let you go. Together with Jean-Claude, you are my life. I can't lose you.'

He was already walking away and as Emily called his name he turned, gripping the bedpost so hard that his knuckles showed white.

'Why did you keep so many secrets?' she asked, desperate to understand. 'What I perceived as your lack of trust in me gave Robyn all the ammunition she needed.'

'*Chérie,* you were so pure, so…innocent. I wanted to protect you especially when I realised I couldn't fight my desperation to make you my wife. Vaillon marriages are not renowned for being happy. It's as if they are cursed and I despised myself for my weakness over you. I should never have married you, *mon ange,*' he finished huskily and the tears slid unchecked down her face.

'Then why did you?' She stared at him, her vulnerability exposed, and he groaned and moved forward as if to take her in his arms. Then he changed his mind and shoved his hands into his pockets.

'Because I love you.' The words seemed to be torn from his throat, as if each syllable was alien and unfamiliar to him, and she had the strangest feeling that he was afraid to look at her. 'I didn't want to,' he admitted, his voice cracking with emotion. '*Mon Dieu,* I know better than most that love hurts. When I first met you I thought I would be content with a brief affair. The chemistry between us was white-hot and I knew you felt it, too,' he told her, and she felt her cheeks flame. 'I hadn't counted on you being quite so innocent and it quickly became clear that the kindest thing I could do, for both our sakes, was walk away.'

'But you didn't,' Emily murmured, her mind still reeling from his startling admission that he loved her. She didn't dare believe him but neither could she ignore the raw emotion in his eyes.

'*Non.* I should have realised then the danger I was in,' he told her ruefully. 'I found that I couldn't leave you any more than I could cut out my own heart. Marriage seemed the only sensible option but even then I kidded myself that I was in control. I arrogantly thought I could have you on my terms, taking everything you gave so sweetly and offering nothing in return except a certain amount of expertise in bed.'

'You certainly gave me that,' Emily muttered, unable to hide her embarrassment as she recalled her wanton response to his passion. 'The only time I ever felt close to you was when we made love, and I clung to the fact that you desired me because I had nothing else of you. When I fell pregnant I took your coldness towards me as rejection and I couldn't bear it. I loved you so much,' she whispered thickly, 'but I never knew how you felt about me and I was so unhappy.'

'*Em-il-y,* don't cry, *ma petite,*' he pleaded as he fell onto the bed and hauled her into his arms. 'I have spent a lifetime hiding what is in my heart, but no more. I would rather die than hurt you. *Je t'aime, mon coeur. Tu es ma vie. Je t'adore.*' He found her mouth in a kiss of such tender passion, such *love,* that words were not necessary and she clung to him as if her life depended on it. 'Forgive me?' he begged, a wealth of emotion in his eyes that were as soft as velvet. She wondered how she could ever have thought him cold. He was burning up for her, his glorious pride abandoned in his need to show the feelings he found so hard to put into words.

'There's nothing to forgive,' she said softly. 'All I ever wanted was your love. Nothing else matters.' She ran the tip of her tongue over her swollen lips, noting the way his eyes darkened as he followed her deliberately provocative gesture. 'I have a feeling I'll no longer be needing this,' she teased, as she lifted the bolster from the middle of the bed and threw it across the room. His mouth curved into a sensual smile that promised heaven.

'You have no idea how close I came to ripping that thing apart, along with the collection of unflattering T-shirts you insisted on wearing to bed,' he confided, as he drew the straps of her nightgown down her arms until her breasts were exposed to his hungry gaze. 'Sleep became an unknown quantity as I fantasised about your body that was only inches from mine but separated by a chasm of misunderstanding. From now on there will be no more secrets between us, *mon amour*,' he insisted, his breath warm on her skin as his mouth followed the path of his hands, and she obligingly lifted her hips so that he could remove her nightgown.

'I love you, Luc,' she told him urgently as he struggled out of his own clothes with a complete lack of finesse that moved her more than anything else had done.

'And I love you, *mon ange*, more than I can ever say,' he assured her huskily, his eyes darkening as he hesitated and eased away from her a fraction. 'I'm not sure we should be doing this,' he muttered, his hand moving to stroke her stomach. 'The baby…'

'Will be fine,' she whispered gently, understanding at last his innermost fears. 'You're not going to make me beg, are you?' she teased, and trembled at the adoration in his eyes as he entered her with exquisite care and began to move in a rhythm that was as old as time.

'I am the one who should beg,' he breathed against her skin, 'for your love.'

'You have it unreservedly,' she murmured, and there was no more time for words as he took them to that place where time ceased to exist and sensation overwhelmed them.

'Are you sure you don't mind about the baby?' Emily asked when they lay replete in each other's arms and he caught the faint hesitancy in her voice. He would spend the rest of his life assuring her of his love, he vowed fiercely. Never again would he give her reason to doubt his adoration for her, Jean-Claude and all their future children.

'My heart is full,' he said simply. 'I never knew I could feel such joy. You, Jean-Claude and this little one—you are my world and I will always be there for you. Especially when you're running a global babywear business,' he added with a smile. 'I love you, *chérie*.' Emily wrapped her arms around his neck.

'I've a feeling I'm going to be fully occupied for quite some while,' she said happily, and his murmur of approval was lost as his lips claimed her in a kiss that spoke louder than words of his love.

They're tall, dark...and ready to marry!

If you love reading about our sensual Italian men, don't delay,
look out for the next story in this great miniseries:

THE ITALIAN'S
FUTURE BRIDE
by Michelle Reid

#2595
On Sale January.

When Rafaelle Villani found himself mistakenly
engaged to innocent blond Englishwoman
Rachel Carmichael, he lost no time in claiming
his fake fiancée. But soon Rachel feared she
had conceived his baby....

Coming in February:
THE ITALIAN'S FORCED BRIDE by Kate Walker

www.eHarlequin.com   HPIH0107

REQUEST YOUR FREE BOOKS!

HARLEQUIN® *Presents* ®

2 FREE NOVELS
PLUS 2
FREE GIFTS!

PASSION GUARANTEED SEDUCTION

HARLEQUIN *Presents*

POSH DOCS

Dedicated, daring and devastatingly
handsome—these doctors are guaranteed
to raise your temperature!

The new collection by your favorite authors,
available in January 2007:

HER BABY SECRET by Kim Lawrence
THE GREEK CHILDREN'S DOCTOR by Sarah Morgan
HER HONORABLE PLAYBOY by Kate Hardy
SHEIKH SURGEON by Meredith Webber